The Ballad of Delta Rose

After more than twenty years of living a life on the road, Delta Rose returns to the ranch he once owned with his fiancée, Etta James. A bullet wedged close to his heart has dealt Delta the dead man's hand.

He soon discovers Etta has a secret: they have a son who, by now a young man, is in trouble. He is charged with both robbery and murder. Can Delta redeem himself for a past ill spent and save the life of the son he never knew he had?

By the same author

The Tarnished Star
Arkansas Smith

The Ballad of Delta Rose

Jack Martin

ROBERT HALE · LONDON

First published in Great Britain 2011

ISBN 978-0-7090-9188-2

Robert Hale Limited
Clerkenwell House
Clerkenwell Green
London EC1R 0HT

www.halebooks.com

Typeset by
Derek Doyle & Associates, Shaw Heath
Printed and bound in Great Britain by
CPI Antony Rowe, Chippenham and Eastbourne

This one's for JD21

*Special thanks go to Dr Keith Souter
for information on the effects of gunshot wounds.*

ONE

Delta Rose only went into the saloon to escape the harsh afternoon sun. He didn't particularly want a drink, he'd never been one for strong liquor and even beer would sit heavy on his stomach. Nor did he feel like eating; he could still taste the dust cloud of a hard journey; it made his throat feel like gravel and he was too bone-weary for good digestion. He most certainly didn't want a gunfight, but that was just what he got.

Feeling beholden to purchase something, Delta walked up to the counter and waited for the barkeep to notice him. It didn't take long for the balding, podgy man to wobble over and smile, his breath offensive on the air.

'A beer,' Delta said.

'Just a beer?' The barkeep smiled.

'Just a beer.'

'A beer it is.' The barkeep smiled again. 'Want anything to eat, stranger?'

'Just a beer,' Delta repeated.

A frown, followed by another of those false smiles.

'Sure thing, stranger.'

'Thank you.'

'You passing through, stranger?'

'Just passing.'

'Most people is these days. Hayes ain't the boom town it once was.'

'Shame about that.'

'Sure is. Take a look around, you. Ain't more than five people here and this is my busy time of the day. 'Course, the place fills up at night but a man can't survive on the night's takings alone. Town used to be bursting with cowboys and traders and pretty girls. Now we're civilized.'

'Nice to be civilized,' Delta said.

'Is it?'

'Thank you for the beer.'

'Welcome, stranger.'

Delta tossed a coin on the counter, waited for his change, then took a stool in the darkest corner of the saloon. He looked around him and counted six people, including himself and the barkeep. This suited him just fine. If this was civilization then more power to it.

He took a sip of the beer and closed his eyes.

Within minutes he was asleep.

Shouting followed by gunfire.

The sound of gunfire can be quite distinct. The roar of a Colt, for instance, is nothing like the crack of a Remington. Furthermore, a Henry sounds nothing like a derringer and, whilst it is true that to the untrained ear a gunshot is a gunshot with no variations in cadence, Delta knew that he was being awakened by the very fierce shout of a Colt.

Delta went from a state of complete sleep to total awareness, within the blink of an eye. He got to his feet and stood there in the darkened corner, body rigid, hands hanging by his side, ready to draw iron.

His eyes narrowed to slits, he looked around the room.

There was a man on the floor; he rolled about sobbing and clutching his arm. Delta could see blood seeping through the man's fingers where he held his arm. Someone had winged him and that someone must have been the young man – man? More a kid really – standing with a smoking Colt in his hand.

The kid's gaze travelled to the gloomy corner and fixed directly upon Delta.

'I got no argument with you, mister,' the kid said.

'Suits me fine,' Delta replied, but he held the kid's stare. Both of them were oblivious to the man on the floor with the shot up arm. The winged man looked from one to the other, spittle and snot over his face, and then went back to his whimpering.

'He drew first,' the kid said, pointing down to the whimpering man at his feet. The man rolled over and tried to scuttle out of harm's way, but he collapsed, yelling out his pain.

'Shut up,' the kid said, his eyes briefly glancing at the wounded man. He returned Delta's gaze and even though his dander was up he felt hesitant. He sure enough didn't want to fight this stranger. 'He drew first,' the kid repeated.

'Ain't none of my business,' Delta replied without taking his eyes off the kid. 'Less you want to make it so.'

The kid shook his head.

At that moment the batwings swung open and a man entered. The man was in his mid fifties but lean and powerful-looking. A shock of silver hair curled under the brim of his hat and he had the bluest eyes imaginable. He wore the badge of the sheriff's office and his rig was hung low on his hip.

'What happened here?' he asked.

Delta relaxed and sat back down. He reached for his beer and took a sip. It had gone flat, but that didn't bother him none.

'He drew first,' the kid said yet again. 'I could have killed him but I didn't.'

'Then put that iron back in leather,' the sheriff said, pointing with the eye of his own Colt.

'Sure thing, Sheriff Masters.' The kid slid the Colt back into its holster and adjusted his belt. He stood there, looking at the sheriff.

The sheriff looked at the man on the floor, then at the kid. 'Harvey,' he shouted and the barkeep yelped from his position behind the counter. 'Is it like the kid says.'

'Sure is, Sheriff Masters,' the barkeep, evidently called Harvey, answered. 'I don't know what went on outside but they came in here arguing. Billings went for his gun first and the kid put one in his shooting arm. Quick as a flash he was.'

'Someone get the doc.' The sheriff took a look around the saloon and for a brief moment his eyes fell on Delta. He frowned and turned back to the kid. 'You'll have to come with me.'

'Why?' the kid protested. 'You heard how it was. I did nothing wrong.'

'That maybe so, but I'll have to take a statement from you.'

'I ain't under arrest?'

'No,' the sheriff said, wearily. 'You ain't under arrest.'

The batwings swung open again and a small, balding man, the doc, Delta guessed, came into the saloon and looked at the man on the floor. He clucked his tongue on the roof of his mouth, then bent to the man and proceeded to administer to his needs. After a moment he stood back up.

'Someone get him over to my place,' the doctor said. 'He can be moved. He's not in any danger of death but I'll have to get that bullet out.'

The sheriff nodded and two men lifted the semi-conscious man from the floor, and dragged him out of the saloon.

The doctor followed behind them.

The sheriff looked at the kid and smiled. 'Wait there,' he said. He walked over to the corner and stood before Delta's table. 'You'll have to come along too.'

'I'm nothing to do with this,' Delta snapped. There was firmness to his voice and a hard edge to his eyes.

'You witnessed it.'

'I was asleep. I saw nothing more than you.'

'Asleep?'

'Yeah, I've been riding some. I was tired and the gunshot woke me.'

'Nevertheless, I'll need to talk to you.'

'What for?'

'You're a stranger in Hayes,' the sheriff said. 'That makes you being here my business. Hayes is a quiet town, we don't allow transients and I like to know what's going on with any newcomers.'

'Friendly little town you got here.'

'I just need to talk to you is all.'

Delta looked across at the kid who was now leaning against a table, watching the exchange with the sheriff.

'Like him,' Delta said, pointing to the kid. 'I ain't under arrest.'

'You ain't under arrest,' the sheriff agreed.

TWO

'That Matt's a good kid but he's gonna get himself in real trouble one day soon,' the sheriff said and sat himself down behind his desk. He took his pipe from the top drawer, filled the bowl with tobacco and sucked it to life. 'Damn shame. The kid hasn't had much of a start in life, what without a pa and his ma having to do everything for him. It's made him tough, maybe too tough.'

'Life's full of sad cases like that,' Delta said.

'Just what we need, another tough kid with a chip on his shoulder.' The sheriff shook his head.

Delta said nothing. If the damn fool kid wanted to tie a noose for himself, then it was none of his concern.

'Twenty-one years old,' the sheriff continued, thoughtfully. 'Be a miracle if he makes twenty-two.'

Again Delta said nothing, just stared at the sheriff, his face expressionless.

'Now what did you say your name was, stranger?' the sheriff asked, speaking through a cloud of pungent burley tobacco smoke.

'I didn't,' Delta said. He had sat here for the last twenty minutes while the sheriff took a statement from the kid and once again he was feeling tired, irritable. The kid had been released and Delta figured there was nothing to keep him here either.

'Then I'm asking.' The sheriff's jaw took on a hard line and his eyes blazed. For all his advanced years he certainly didn't seem the sort of man to take too much nonsense.'

'Delta.'

'Any more name?'

'Just Delta.'

'You from down South?'

Delta's eyes narrowed. 'I was,' he said.

'Well, Mr Delta, do you want to tell me your business in Hayes?'

'I've got no business here. I was just passing through on my way someplace else. It's been a long ride and I needed to get out of the sun.'

The sheriff nodded. 'Then you'll be moving on?'

'I will.'

'When?'

Delta didn't much like the sheriff's tone but he decided it wasn't worth kicking up a fuss. He had hoped on maybe taking a bed in town for the night, before moving off in the morning, but all of a sudden that didn't seem such a good idea. He didn't have too far to go now, maybe another ten miles or so, and riding out immediately would sure avoid any potential trouble. There was also the possibility that someone in town, one of the old timers, someone who had been here when the town was nothing more than a saloon and a cathouse, would recognize him and that word would reach Etta that he was back.

'Just as soon as I finish with you.' Delta reached into his shirt and took out the makings. Without asking permission, he rolled a cigarette and stuck it between his lips.

The sheriff struck a match against his desk and held it out for Delta.

'Well,' the sheriff said, following a short silence while both men smoked. 'I guess there's no reason for me to detain you. I won't pry any further.'

'Good.'

'But I should warn you.'

'Warn me?'

The sheriff removed the pipe from his mouth and used it to illustrate his point, jabbing it in the air as he spoke. 'You're a stranger, you wear your guns tied down low like a gunslinger. I've got nothing at all against that but if you sling your guns around, I'd prefer you didn't do it in Hayes.'

'I'm not a gunfighter,' Delta said firmly. 'And I don't intend slinging my guns here or anyplace else.'

'Good. Then you're free to leave town, stranger.'

'You running me out of town?'

'Not unless I need to.'

Delta stood up and looked down at the sheriff. The lawman seemed mighty sure of himself; at the moment he looked perfectly relaxed, but Delta had the feeling the lawman would be able to spring into action in an instant should the need arise. Here was a man he could respect and he certainly didn't want any trouble with the law. Whilst it was true he hadn't done anything, had as much right as the next man to go where he damn well pleased in this country, he figured he'd move on in any case. There was no money to be made here and he'd been run out of better towns that this in the past.

It made no difference to him.

Indeed the only reason he'd stopped here in the first place had been curiosity. Twenty odd years ago the town hadn't really been here and the Hayes Cattle Company had owned the land upon which it sat. Other than the town's name Delta had seen no signs that the Hayes Company still operated here.

'I'll be leaving of my own accord,' Delta said. 'I've got business elsewhere in any case.'

'Good. Then you're free to go, stranger.'

Delta didn't leave town immediately, though.

Straight from the sheriff's office he'd gone back to the saloon and, suddenly hungry, ordered himself a meal and a pot of coffee. He devoured the meat and potatoes quickly, attacking the food like a man who had no idea where his next meal was coming from, which, Delta supposed, wasn't too far from the truth. He mopped the gravy with a lump of stale bread, leaving the plate cleaner than washing ever could and drained the entire pot of coffee. The meal had cost well over the odds but it had tasted good enough. Directly afterwards he paid for a bath, but before taking it he had gone and checked on his horse at the livery stable, ordering it to be given extra grain and to be brushed down thoroughly.

And now, just as night was falling, man and horse were fresh and eager to move on from this unfriendly little town. Delta tipped his hat to the sheriff as he rode along the main street.

'Be seeing you, stranger,' the sheriff said, tipping his own hat.

Delta smiled. 'I sure hope not.'

He spurred the horse forward and left town in a cloud of dust.

THREE

Delta covered close on five miles before making camp for the night.

He knew that if he kept on riding he would reach the ranch in no time, but he didn't want to come upon the place during the night. That was liable to rattle Etta and he was unsure of the reception he would get in any case, so it made sense to play it safe. Best to ride up on the ranch nice and easy with the sun behind him. And besides that he was aching, the slug he carried inside him was giving him trouble again; the upper left side of his body was numbed. He needed to bed himself down, to keep still, and not be jostled about in the saddle.

He didn't set a fire, not that he would have been up to the task in any case. Just tethered the horse to a cottonwood, laid his bedroll on the ground and stretched out on his back, the only position he was ever able to sleep these days. He drew in deep, slow breaths – the way the doctor had told him, and gradually feeling returned to his left side, bringing with it a throb that felt like an earthquake within his ribcage. Bad as it was, though, the pain was preferable to the paralysis. There were times when the bullet would affect his vocal chords, leaving him mute for days on end. He would also suffer from episodic fevers and fatigue and it was a miracle he had survived thus far.

He lay there, knowing that eventually the pain would subside – either that or it would kill him. There was nothing he could do other than remain still and breathe deeply, all the while hoping for the best. Completely fill his lungs and then allow then to deflate gently while he willed the pain to pass.

The bullet had been with him for almost two years now and he was amazed that he had survived this long, but he didn't think that would be the case for much longer. Each time the slug shifted inside him, moved that little closer to his heart, he expected that that would be the time he died.

For the moment, though, he lived but, as a gambler, he recognized the cards fate had dealt him. He was holding the dead man's hand and it was merely a question of how long the game would take to play out.

After some time he closed his eyes and soon he was asleep.

Delta woke with first light. He was up and about in time to watch the show as the sky transformed from the inky blackness of night to the purple patchwork of dawn, and then on to the brilliant blue of day. In the distance Delta heard the gentle cry of a hawk as it searched for a morning meal. It was a sight that only a man living on borrowed time could truly appreciate. With death peering over a man's shoulder, its icy breath felt on the back of a man's neck, everything was enhanced. The cobalt sky was saturated and the landscape vividly exaggerated. The sun, now rising in the sky, looked as if a child's hand, smiley face and all, had painted it there.

He pulled his coat tighter around him and took the makings from his pocket. Soon he had a smoke going and he took a swig of water from the canteen that hung on his saddle-bags. He thought about getting a fire going, boiling up some coffee before he moved on but then he didn't figure it was worth it. He didn't have far to go now and the thought of seeing Etta again made him eager to move out. Even if he weren't exactly sure what sort of reception he would get.

He filled a nosebag with oats and gave them to the horse, allowing the beast to eat its fill while he busied himself with folding his bedroll and tying it to the saddle. And then, the oats consumed, he spurred the horse off in a gentle walk towards the distant hills, beyond which Etta had made her home among the redwood trees she so loved.

Delta tried to picture how Etta would look now. It had been more than twenty years since he'd last seen her, twenty long, hard years. Would age have withered her beauty? He didn't think that was possible. Sure, life would have left lines on that once smooth skin, maybe robbed her eyes of some of their vitality, but Etta held a very special beauty that could not be spoilt with the passage of time. Her beauty was more than physical. It came from within, a radiance that positively shone in her eyes.

Delta shook his head, amused by the poetic thoughts. He guessed he was getting soft in his old age. He was about to speed the horse up when he heard a sound, a voice maybe, that caused him to pull the horse back, stopping it dead.

He patted the side of its head while he listened.

'Good girl,' he whispered to his horse and cocked his head, almost like an animal, while he strained to hear anything else. All that greeted him, other than the sounds of nature itself, was complete silence. All the same he knew he hadn't imagined it. It had been faint and indistinct but there had been no mistaking it. There was not an iota of doubt within Delta's mind that he had heard a voice, a human voice.

Delta climbed carefully from the saddle, removed his rifle from the boot and allowed the horse to graze amongst the foliage. Ahead of him, beyond the tree line was a clearing sloping gently towards the valley below, which was where, Delta, figured, the voice had originated. He cautiously moved forward until he reached the clearing. He looked out across a field of tall grasses that sloped gently to the east.

Delta stood there for a moment and was just about to turn back to his horse when he heard it again. This time there was no mistaking the voice and there were several, all of them male. He couldn't make out what was being said but he fancied he heard at least four distinct voices. This was none of his business and he had no desire to make it so, but he held the rifle across his body and carefully walked out into the clearing. There was no harm in taking a quick look, if only to establish whether the voices represented a threat.

Whoever the voices belonged to they were, so far, unaware of Delta's presence.

Delta felt he would like it to remain that way.

He'd take a quick look and then ride on.

FOUR

'No killing,' Matt said and tightened his bandanna around the lower half of his face so that only his eyes were visible beneath the brim of his hat. 'We do this without killing anyone.'

Rile shifted in his saddle. He liked to think of himself as the leader of this little gang. At twenty-three he was, after all, the eldest of the four men and the fact that he had already done two years in the territorial prison gave him some authority. He was a hard knock while the other three men were little more than greenhorns.

'Not gonna play chicken on us, I hope?' Rile said, sneering in Matt's direction. He flapped, chicken-style, with his arms and made comical clucking sounds. His horse shifted, uneasy at the tomfoolery.

'I ain't no chicken,' Matt snapped.

The remaining two men – Hayloft, twenty one years old, hailing from Arkansas, and Clement, just tipped twenty, hailed from God alone knew where – watched the exchange with some amusement.

Rile scratched his forehead and then spat in the dirt. 'Well,' he said. 'Some desperadoes we are.'

'Let's just get this done.' Matt said. There was firmness in his voice and it was clear that he didn't much like Rile and wasn't trying to hide it. The two men looked at each other and all of a sudden it was as if they were out here alone, their two companions became spectators on the sideline, almost existing in a different reality. Rile and Matt seemed to be locked in some mental struggle as they held each other's gaze.

It was Rile who broke first. He looked away at the far horizon and then shook his head with a chuckle born of bravado. If he had been honest with himself he would have to admit that the kid made him more than a little uneasy. Maybe he'd put a bullet in the runt's back one day soon.

'Come on,' he said and spurred his horse into an immediate gallop.

Delta watched them ride off until they disappeared from view into the valley below. Only then did he return to his horse and ride off towards Etta's place. When he came out of the forest and into the opening, the sun was high in the sky, and Delta was grateful for the feeling of warmth upon his face as he rode.

The more Delta thought about it, the more he was sure that one of the four men had been the gun slinging kid from town. He wasn't exactly able to swear his life on it, the men had been too far away to make a positive identification with the naked eye, but one of them had sure enough looked like the kid.

It mattered not, Delta thought. It was none of his business and when the men had ridden off in the opposite direction, then that was the end of it. Delta had his own business to contend with and whatever the four men had been up to was not his concern.

This was a glorious part of the country. Now that he had left the forest behind and was travelling across open country the vistas opening up before him were stunning. About 300 yards ahead of him he could see Clawson's Creek, its waters glistening with captured sunlight and beyond that the white grasses of the flatlands stretched towards the distant hills. It was a panorama that no mortal artist could ever hope to capture, no matter how skilled in the use of charcoal or oils. There had to be a divine hand behind this creation.

Behind those distant hills stood Etta's place.

It all looked so new, fresh, as if it was virgin land and he was seeing it for the first time, but Delta had been here before. Once he had even considered settling here, putting down roots, and he had done that for some time, but eventually the wanderlust had grown within him. He had become like a trapped animal and he turned his back on a life of domesticity. He had been younger then, impossibly young, and he often regretted the decision made all those years ago, wondered how different his life would have been had he stayed here with Etta and carved out a life from the land.

One thing was certain – he wouldn't be carrying a bullet around inside him. No, he thought. He'd probably be dead already. Worked to death, back broken by the daily toil and the only reward a pauper's grave. Delta smiled grimly. That was his old way of thinking, a young man's mind, a young man's thoughts. It was that way of thinking that had set him off on the life of a drifter, plying his trade (gambling) in frontier town after frontier town, always looking for that big win, that hand that would change his life. Only it never did come and when – if – it did then it changed lives sure enough, only not necessarily for the better.

Delta had always intended to return to Etta and he'd known that one day he would. In his mid-twenties anything had seemed possible and he was sure it wouldn't be too many years before he came home to Etta and the farm, untold riches in his saddle-bags. But his thirties came and went in a whirl of gambling, prospecting, gunfighting and even, at one point, bounty hunting. And now he was firmly in his forties, had the beginnings of a paunch, grey hair and his ears and nose had the annoying tendency to sprout spindly white hairs.

Oh, and let's not forget the bullet lodged inside him, too close to the heart to be removed.

No, let's not forget that.

'What's done is done,' Delta said, patting the side of the horse's head. 'Ain't no changing the past, girl.' All the same if he'd had his life to live over again he would have done things differently, of that he was sure.

Hindsight though, was a wonderful thing.

FIVE

Delta pulled on the reins, bringing the horse to a stop. He looked down into the valley and there was the ranch he'd turned his back on so many years ago. Etta had certainly been prosperous in his absence. When he'd left it had been just the house itself and the barn but now there were several outbuildings, and a new wing had been added to the ranch house itself, making it look like a small-scale version of some of the mansions down South. There was a huge corral, which at the moment housed maybe a dozen horses. To the left of the corral Delta could make out tiny specks, shifting about the ground like ants. He took these to be chickens or at least fowl of some kind, but from this distance it was difficult to tell for certain. And there were several busy-looking human figures dashing hither and thither. He could see one man approaching a horse in the corral, swinging a rope above his head. He watched while the man lassoed the horse and wrestled it to the ground. A puff of dust, barely visible to Delta, erupted into the air.

He didn't think anyone had noticed him yet, but Delta fully expected someone to look up and see him as he spurred his horse down the hill. The farm had been built in a natural valley, the redwood-dotted hills around it giving it protection from the worse of the elements. In the heat of summer the hills provided shade and in the winter warmth, and Delta had to pick his way carefully as he negotiated the horse down the steep banking. There was a well-worn path that snaked down the hill, a more gradual incline, maybe fifty feet away but, contrary as ever, Delta took some satisfaction in entering by the more arduous route.

He was, at least, consistent since the arduous route was the way he had lived his life.

Steve Carter, the ranch foreman, noticed the rider first. He looked up from the fence he had been repairing and pointed to the man who was bringing his horse down an incline that was so steep, it was almost vertical.

'Damn fool's gonna break his neck,' he said, thoughtfully.

O'Dowde, a swarthy-looking Irishman, came over and stood besides his boss. He removed his rawhide gloves and wiped his brow. 'Who the hell is that?'

'Damned if I know,' Steve said, speaking through clenched teeth. He had to shield his eyes from the sun to follow the rider's progress down the hill.

'Damn loco fool whoever it is.'

'Sure can handle a horse, though,' the Irishman said. 'Takes some skill with an animal to persuade it to come down that hill like that.'

'More stupidity than skill,' Steve said and wiped his own brow. By now the mysterious rider had gained everyone's attention and Steve barked out an order for the men to get back to work. He threw down his own tools and walked over towards the stream, going to meet the rider should he complete his perilous journey.

Which the rider did and Steve made eye contact with the man as the horse took the last few feet towards flatter ground. At the bottom of the hill the rider patted the horse's head, whispered some soothing words, then trotted over to where the man stood besides stream.

'Howdy,' Delta said.

'Howdy.' Steve tipped his hat. 'You know you're on private property, stranger?'

Delta nodded.

'Yeah,' he said. He took a look around him, marvelling at how much the ranch had grown since he'd last seen it. The ranch house itself had looked impressive from atop the rise but here, up close, it was breathtaking. And the horses in the enclosure all looked to be magnificent, expensive creatures. Like the thoroughbreds Delta had seen at the racetracks back East.

'Where you heading?' Steve asked.

Delta smiled. 'Here,' he said. 'Right here.'

Steve looked at the man with puzzlement and Delta was sure he saw him tense. He's getting ready to draw, Delta thought. If I provoke him in any way he'll reach for iron. The wild old days had gone now and the world was moving on, but men could still be over-fond of going for a gun.

'I'm here to see Etta,' Delta said at last.

'Miss James?' Steve asked. 'What business could you have with Miss James.'

Delta smiled. Miss James, so Etta had never married. Although he supposed it was possible she was a widow and had reverted to her maiden name.

'Who are you?' Delta asked.

'I'm the ranch foreman,' Steve said. 'And I think you should explain who you are.'

'Tell Etta that's Delta's here.'

'Delta?'

'Yeah, Delta. That's me.'

'Well I sure as hell ain't going to bother Miss James without a little more information than that.'

'What else do you need?' Delta shifted in his saddle. He felt a twinge in his side and hoped this didn't signify another of his paralysis attacks. The last thing he needed at the moment was to fall from his horse and be spread out there on the ground like a cripple. Fine homecoming that would be, him turning up here after all these years and all he'd be able to do was blink his eyes.

'Just tell Etta what I've said. That'll be enough.'

'I'll be dammed if I will,' Steve said. 'And where's this Etta business come from? It's Miss James. Who the hell are you?'

'Delta will be enough.' Delta insisted.

Before anything else could be said Delta looked beyond the man and saw a female figure coming towards them. He knew it was Etta immediately, from the proud way she held herself as she approached them. The closer she approached the slower and steadier her steps became as it dawned on her who the newcomer astride the horse was.

Steve turned to see Etta approach and when he looked back at the man on the horse he could see that he did indeed know Etta James. There was a smile on his lips and a look of recognition in his eyes that bothered the ranch foreman. Who was this stranger? And what did he mean to Miss James?

The woman called Etta James came within ten feet of them and then stopped dead in her tracks. The look on her face, first of shock, was soon replaced by a tight smile, but then anger turned up in her eyes. She shook her head, as if disbelieving whom she was seeing, then her mouth pulled so tight that it seemed to close up, looking like a scar upon her face.

'Etta,' Delta said and tipped his hat. He looked at her in the way a starving man would look at a hearty meal, his eyes greedily taking in every feature and he saw not one, but two women standing before him. He saw Etta as she was now, a little older maybe but still as beautiful as ever, but he also saw the girl she had once been. That young, insanely gorgeous girl he had known so many years ago peered out from behind her eyes.

'What's going on here?' Steve asked, turning back to his employer. 'Do you know this man, Miss James?'

Etta nodded and took another step towards Delta. She was carrying a wicker trug, lavender leaves poking untidily over its edge and a pruning knife resting on the freshly cut stems. She stood stock-still for a moment, then dropped the trug, spilling its fragrant contents over the ground.

'Delta,' she said and fainted clean away.

SIX

'They came tearing out of the brush, pistols shooting, lead flying everywhere,' Clift said, gesturing widely with his arms. He swallowed noisily, his dry throat rasping and looked nervously at his boss. 'There was nothing we could do. They shot Willy's hat clean off his head, the bullet damn near parted his hair.'

'And where's Willy now?' Maxwell King asked, in that cultured English accent of his. It was a very specific accent: middle England.

Clift shrugged his shoulders.

'He. . . .' he said. His word crippled, stumbled about on his tongue, unable to find voice. Eventually he managed to blurt out that his partner had run off.

Maxwell King closed his eyes for a moment, which caused all the men around him suddenly to feel nervous. When he acted like this there was no way of predicting which way he would go. He almost went into a trance, entering a private world wholly his own and when he emerged from the fugue he could be calm, relaxed and philosophical. He could also, and more often if the truth be told, be angry – murderously so.

'How many?' he asked.

'Four,' Clift said, his voice again feeble and seeming to struggle from his throat. 'They took us by surprise. We couldn't do nothing, Mr King, honest we couldn't.'

'So they got away with my money,' King said. 'A month's wages for almost fifty men. A sizeable amount.'

Clift nodded and mouthed a silent prayer beneath his breath. He tensed when he saw King's hand reaching for the top drawer in his desk. The drawer where he kept his gun.

'Any idea who the bandits were?' King asked and slid the drawer open. His hand hovered over the Webley pistol like a dragonfly contemplating a kill.

'They wore masks, bandannas pulled over their faces. I told you that.'

'How would they know you were carrying so much money? Did you speak to anyone in town?'

'No, sir,' Clift said. 'I'm not stupid enough to go shouting my mouth off.'

'What about Willy?'

'Willy?'

'Did he go shouting his mouth off?'

'No, sir. Willy wouldn't do a thing like that. We do this run every month, that's no secret. Maybe they've been watching us, you know. It's also no secret how many men you employ here and you're known to be wealthy.'

'Then why did Willy run off?' King asked, speaking in the way a man would when trying to reason with a child. He kept his voice level and his words were searching, in the way a surgeon's knife probes a wound.

'He . . .' Clift said and once again became tongue-tied. He looked heavenwards and made a silent prayer beneath his breath. 'He was scared of you, Mr King,' he said at last. 'Of what you would do to us.'

'What did he think I'd do?' King asked and looked at the other men in the room, smiling as if what Clift had said was absurd. Why should any of his men fear him?

'I sure as hell don't know,' Clift said and looked at the two men standing behind him. The two men were known as Cade and Miller and no one was quite sure what their duties were around here, only that they were always with King. He seldom went anywhere without the two men by his side.

'All I know,' King said, 'is that you picked my money up from the bank this morning and now it's gone and Willy's gone too. And you've no idea who took it or where Willy is.'

'They wore bandannas. I told you that.'

'So you did,' King said and smiled. 'And Willy ran off, you also told me that.'

Clift nodded.

'Was Willy in on this robbery, do you think?' King asked.

'No, sir,' Clift said firmly. 'I do not think that was so. Willy wouldn't do that.'

Then King pulled the Webley from the drawer and coldly shot Clift. The man had worked for him for over ten years, but at this moment King would have shot his own brother if he had stood before him. He watched as Clift was thrown backwards, a jagged obscenity opening in his chest, to crash against the door and slide down it, getting closer to death with each and every inch. King leaned forward in his chair, watching as Clift's body twitched its final death throes. Then he blew the smoke from the barrel of his gun like a dime-novel gunfighter.

Cade and Miller didn't even look at Clift. They continued to stare forward, faces as expressionless as lobotomized sheep.

'Stick him in one of the barns,' King said, and returned the gun to the drawer. He didn't speak to either of the two men in particular but both nodded eagerly like a pair of dogs eager to please their master. 'Then fetch the sheriff while I clean this place up.'

Both men did then look at each other, each willing the other to question their boss. It was the taller of the two men, the one known as Cade, who spoke. He looked for a second at Clift's body, then turned to his boss.

'The sheriff?'

'Indeed,' King said. 'Clift was shot in the robbery. Rode in here all bloodied and didn't last no longer than to tell us what happened. The sheriff will need to find whoever did this. And when you're in town find Willy and keep him out of harm's way until I've seen the sheriff. Find out if he's talked to anyone about the robbery, find out just what he's told them.'

'Yes, sir,' Cade said and nudged his companion. Together they slid Clift's body away from the door so that they could open it. His sightless eyes rolled back in his head. Between them they lugged the body out into the pale morning sunshine.

SEVEN

'You can sleep in the barn,' Etta said and smiled. 'There's no room in the bunkhouse and besides I don't think the men have taken to you.'

Delta wanted to ask about the man called Steve. Was he more than the ranch foreman? But he decided it was none of his business. 'The barn'll suit me just fine.'

'I'll get some blankets and a lantern from the house,' Etta said.

Delta looked at the barn. It was a solid construction, well built and had survived many harsh winters with nary a blemish to its timbers. He had built it himself during the last summer he'd spent here. It all seemed so long ago now and yet the barn looked as if it had been built but one or two years ago.

'It's survived well,' he said.

'You built it on sturdy foundations,' Etta said. 'Far sturdier than those that you walk upon.'

'You saying I've got wayward feet?'

'No, not your feet,' Etta said and took a long hard

look at the barn, perhaps remembering the man Delta had been when he'd built it. 'I'm saying you've got a wayward soul.'

'Wayward soul.' Delta smiled, seeming to contemplate while he took the makings from his rawhide pouch and threw together a smoke. 'Etta James, even your insults have a poetry about them.'

'I call it *Ode to a Rotten Man,*' she said, teasing Delta. She was amazed at how comfortable she felt at his side. Even after all this time apart she felt she knew this man better than any other. It was as if they had never been apart.

'I guess I deserve that.' Delta hissed smoke out between his lips. 'I surely do.'

'You sway in the wind,' Etta said. 'That's all.'

Above them a hawk sounded but it was not a hunting call, it was softer than that and strangely melodic. It was, Delta thought, as if the bird was calling for its mate, singing its desires and sending them forth on the wind. The sun dropped, creating mood as shadows made the vastness of the land somehow intimate. It was as if nature itself had decided to display its own poetry.

They had spent the day together. Etta had taken Delta around the ranch, showing him how it had increased both in size and stock. Since he had last been here she'd added several acres of land to the ranch, and was now the third biggest landowner in the area. All in all, the land she owned was so big it would take a full day to ride across. She employed a dozen men full time and more than double that number for seasonal work. She had a beef contract with the army that was proving more profitable year after year. All in all life had been pretty good and Delta was fully aware of the irony in the situation. Once he had been a part of all this, but he'd left looking for a fortune. He'd returned carrying not gold but lead and Etta had formed a golden land of her own.

During their ride they had talked over many things, but it had been mostly small-talk; Delta would compliment her on how well she was looking and she would laugh and say he looked as much as ever, whatever that meant. Delta wondered whether she had ever married but he didn't feel it polite to address the subject. True, she still used her family name but there must have been men. In twenty odd years there must have been men, but he kept the question to himself, knowing that it was none of his business. Not to mention a sure quick way for a man to get his face slapped. When he'd turned his back on all this he had relinquished any hold he might have had over Etta James. They hadn't been married, but they were lovers true enough. And it was understood that they would tie the knot one day.

He'd turned his back on all that.

It was too late now.

'The barn'll do fine,' Delta said once again.

'Come up to the house for supper.' Etta tightened the ribbon in her hair. It had blown loose during the ride. The motion exposed the side of her neck and at that moment Delta felt regret for the foolishness of the past like never before. It burned like a fire in the centre of his chest and radiated outwards in molten ripples.

'You don't mind?'

'I wouldn't have offered if I did.'

'No,' Delta said. 'Of course not.'

'That's settled then.'

Delta nodded and turned on his heel, heading towards the barn, but Etta called him back. He spun, dust puffing up at his feet, looking at her.

'Can I ask you something?' she asked.

'Sure.'

'Why have you come back? After all these years, why have you come back?'

'You want the truth?' Delta asked.

'Of course.'

For a moment Delta thought about telling her about the bullet he carried inside him, about the fact that he had come here to die, to spend his last days, *he was sure these were his last days,* with the woman he had once loved, the only woman he had ever truly loved. The woman he still loved in as much of a way as Delta Rose could love.

Instead he simply smiled, shook his head and said: 'I don't rightly know.'

EIGHT

'Should we go to the sheriff in any case?' Miller asked.

'I don't rightly know,' Cade said. They had spent the entire day looking for Willy but the varmint seemed to have vanished. And whilst it was true that Mr King had ordered them to inform the sheriff of the robbery they'd feel a lot safer doing so if they had Willy tucked away safe from harm. The last thing they needed was for him to pop up and start contradicting King's story. 'We take one last look for Willy first, maybe.'

Miller nodded. 'Maybe that is the prudent thing to do.'

'The saloon,' Cade pointed to the Double Diamond and Miller nodded. They had already been here once today in search of Willy, several hours ago, but when they had failed to find him they had ridden back out of town to check the missing man's other haunts. Now they were running out of options and they had no idea where Willy could be hiding out.

They were starting to think that Clift had been wrong and that Willy had been an inside man during the robbery. Maybe he was hidden out somewhere with the owlhoots.

'If he ain't in there,' Cade said, 'we'll go to the sheriff.'

'Take a quick drink first.'

'Sure.'

'No harm in that.'

'None whatsoever.'

They walked, side by side, across the street and into the saloon.

Matt crossed the street and quickly ducked into the alleyway between the livery stable and the forge. He peered around the corner of the stable and watched the two men, King's men, cross the street and enter the Double Diamond, pushing the batwings open with force.

Matt hugged the wall for a moment, pondering what to do. By now news of the robbery would have reached King and he'd had plenty of time to react: almost a full day, and yet nothing had seemed to have happened. The sheriff hadn't left town all day, no posse had been formed, and no news had come that the wage wagon had been robbed. Matt had been in town all afternoon and he would have known about it if anything had happened.

It was all mighty strange and now two of King's men had arrived. Rather than visit the sheriff they'd gone straight into the saloon. Hayloft and Clement were in there and Matt was grateful that they didn't have any of the money to throw around. Directly following the robbery they had ridden to Whispering Rock and hidden the entire haul. They had all agreed that the money would be recovered and split four ways after a suitable period of time had elapsed. All they had to do was keep their mouths shut and live each day as they always had. If they were careful they would be four rich men not too many months from now.

All the same Matt felt his stomach churn. King's men, Matt knew them, if not by name then by sight, knew they were a pair of bruisers. In the past he had seen them pushing people around at King's orders and he knew they could be vicious.

He had to go into the saloon, see what they were doing, what they were saying and make sure Hayloft or Clement didn't do anything to direct suspicion in their direction. At least that hothead Rile wasn't about, Matt thought, thankful for small mercies. That particular varmint had disappeared into the cathouse on the outskirts of town and, Matt knew, he wouldn't turn up until well after dark. It was Rile he would have to watch. He could be a braggart and treated life as if it was a game to be won or lost with wild abandon.

He glanced up and down the street, then stepped out. It was quiet, the only sound being the laughter and the plink of the badly tuned piano that sounded out from the saloon. Matt crossed quickly and stepped through the Double Diamond's batwings.

It was business as usual at the Double Diamond. The piano player, a friendly looking Negro, whom everyone called Sam, was coaxing the best tune he could out of the antiquated instrument, while a saloon girl stood besides him, shaking to the rhythm.

She was merely going through the motions, her heart was not in her performance. Nevertheless a couple of cowboys were shouting their encouragement, cheers peppered with the odd crude remark. There were several men leaning against the counter, Hayloft, Clement and King's men among them. The barkeep was topping up glass after glass with strong liquor and frowning as he tried to answer all the calls for his service. The woman at the piano started warbling and the barkeep threw a spit rag at her.

'Quit your racket,' he shouted. 'And help me out.'

'Harvey,' she shouted back, as the rag landed at her feet.

The woman smiled at the transfixed cowboys, shrugged her shoulders and made her way behind the counter. Sam kept on plinking away but without the woman he had lost his audience.

Matt pushed his way to the counter and nudged in between Hayloft and Clement. Neither of the men protested. Hayloft smiled, took a gulp of his beer and asked if Matt wanted a drink.

'Thanks,' Matt said. 'A beer.' He peered across at King's men, both of them seemed lost in thought. They nursed a shot glass each and neither of them seemed in the mood for conversation.

'Forget that beer.' Matt pulled Hayloft's arm down

before he could get any service. 'We best get out of here.'

'What?' Clement protested. 'I only just started enjoying myself.'

'Come on,' Matt said, keeping his voice low. He pointed his eyes towards King's men.

'They on to us?' Hayloft asked.

'Keep it down,' Matt said. 'Come on, we'll talk outside.'

Once again he cast a look at King's men and a shiver ran the length of his spine. He felt the hairs at the nape of his neck rise and he had to will himself to calm down. He had been worried about the other men somehow giving the game away, either by stupid bragging or losing nerve when the going got tough, and yet here he was at the first hurdle acting like an old woman.

It didn't even represent a hurdle, not really. He had no idea why King's men were here and why there had been no fuss made about the robbery. The only thing he did know was that he needed to calm down; all the same, King's men unnerved him.

'Come on,' he said again. 'Drink up.'

Hayloft and Clement looked at each other for a moment, then both men shrugged their shoulders in a single synchronized move. They drained their respective glasses and allowed Matt to lead the way.

They had reached the batwings, Matt in the lead, when Willy suddenly stumbled in. He fell against Matt and breathed whiskey fumes directly into the young man's face. He squinted his eyes at Matt and for one awful moment the kid thought Willy knew he was one of the men who had robbed the wagon this very morning, but Willy simply smiled and begged his pardon.

Matt steadied Willy as he stepped aside to allow the drunken man to pass. For a moment it was as if the drunken man was using Matt as a dancing partner and they did a merry jig before separating.

'Begging your pardon,' Willy said, slurring his words. He removed his battered hat and poked his finger through the bullet hole, waggling it about as though only noticing the hole for the first time. 'Begging Willy's pardon. Willy's had one darn terrible day, sure enough. Why this morning—' but before Willy could say any more one of King's men came forward and pistol-whipped him to the floor.

Then all hell broke loose.

NINE

Matt was sure Hayloft drew first; spooked by the sudden movement from King's man, he pulled his Colt Navy and let off a wild shot that hit no one, but came perilously close to ending the piano player's career. Even so the musician didn't miss a note and kept on plinking away.

Matt saw the man, who only seconds ago had pistol-whipped Willy, bring up his own weapon in Hayloft's direction, but the kid was quicker and Matt shot. As usual his aim was perfect. The slug entered King's man just below the chin and spiralled upwards through his head to emerge in a spray of crimson from his skull. At first the man didn't seem to realize he was dead and he raised his gun once more, looking a ghastly sight as blood congealed in sightless eyes, before he collapsed, lifeless.

The dead man's companion roared from the counter and pulled a pair of fine-looking pistols. His first shot took Hayloft in the chest, spinning him around, before he collapsed on top of a table. The second flew past Matt's head, so close that the young man felt the heat of its tail.

'Get down,' Matt yelled. In one fluid movement he upended a table and pulled Clement down beside him. The saloon suddenly erupted with panicked yelling and screaming and, absurdly, the constant plink of the piano. Like the captain of his own ship, Sam refused to leave his post. People ran every which way, trying to escape the line of fire.

Only moments ago the saloon had been in full swing but now it had been turned into a battlefield; two men were already dead and the stench of cordite hung in the air like an oppressive cloud. Everyone was going for the batwings of the narrow doorway, but the problem was they were all going at the same time and stumbling over each other. One man struck back when someone pushed an elbow into his throat, only to discover he had just punched out his own brother. All the same, it didn't stop the man stamping all over him as another shot roared inside the room.

Matt peered over the table, looking for a target, but King's man had moved and he couldn't see him amongst the general chaos. Matt spotted him just in time to get his head down as a bullet struck the corner of the table they were using as a barricade, sending wood splinters into the air. Matt fired back but without aiming, the shot intended to give them time to move.

Matt looked at Clement and made a signal for him to run to the door, but the plan changed when King's man struck home with a shot that kissed Clement directly between the eyes: intimate as hell it romanced the man clean into the other world where Hayloft was already waiting for him. Matt watched his friend's head snap back and felt the warm splatter of blood on his own face.

'Clem,' he yelled but it was too late and his friend was beyond the point of hearing. He noticed Willy crawling along the floor, making for the door, and he tried to reach out to stop him when a volley of shots forced him to get back down. Someone's heel struck him a stinging blow to the side of the head, but they ran on oblivious.

Matt cursed beneath his breath as he saw Willy vanish through the door. He knew his only chance was making the outside world himself. King's man was a deadly shot and although Matt wasn't exactly sure where the man was positioned he knew that if he raised his head to find out it would be goodnight. He had to get to the door. King's man must be somewhere by the far end of the counter and as soon as all these people got out of the way he would have a clear shot at the table, filling it full of holes. The thin wood would offer scant protection from the hot lead and Matt realized that if he didn't move fast it would be all over for him.

It was now or never.

Before the rest of the frenzied crowd escaped the building.

He decided he'd come up shooting, hope for the best and dive into the crowd who were currently fighting to get through the batwings. Matt took in a deep breath, all the while wishing the piano player would give it a rest, and suddenly leapt to his feet. Shooting in the general direction of the counter, he made a run towards the door. Rolling himself into a ball, he threw himself towards the feet of the people in the doorway.

An orgy of arms and legs came spilling through the batwings in a manic obscenity, to land in an ungodly mess at the sheriff's feet. The lawman was carrying a Spencer rifle and he held it, resting on his hip, as he stepped into the saloon.

Matt got immediately to his feet as soon as Sheriff Masters disappeared; he felt it prudent to get the hell out of here while he had the chance. He took a look up and down the street for Willy but the varmint had vanished. Why had King's man suddenly pistol-whipped him like that, provoking that darn shooting match? Both Clement and Hayloft were dead, not to mention the man who had done the pistol-whipping.

There would be time enough later to dwell on such matters; Matt knew that any moment now the sheriff would emerge, looking for him. There would be plenty of witnesses who would state that Matt's gang fired first. For now the only option was to vanish. He needed time to gather his thoughts while he figured what the hell to do next.

Matt ran across the street to where he had tethered his horse. Within seconds he had mounted the magnificent pure white thoroughbred and was galloping towards the whorehouse on the outskirts of town. He had to tell Rile what had just happened and, together, the two of them had to get the hell away from Hayes, maybe even the territory.

'You say you work for Maxwell King?' Sheriff Masters lowered the Spencer and rested it in the crook his arm.

'Joshua Cade is my name and that there,' he pointed to his pard's body, 'was Samuel Miller, a fine Texan, murdered right here in this saloon not moments ago.'

'And the other two stiffs, they did some of the killing?'

'They did. My pard got one and I got the other. The third one ran like a yellow coward.'

The lawman bent and picked up an upturned stool and set it right. He sat himself down on it, crossed his legs and laid his rifle across his lap. He had just listened to the man called Cade's version of what had happened. He had been told that they had ridden into town to report the hold-up of King's wage wagon, which had apparently occurred earlier this morning. They had come into the saloon for a drink, 'to ease our dry throats', Cade had said, when the shotgun rider (Willy) on the robbed wagon came in. Willy'd been missing since the robbery and apparently Maxwell King felt he may have taken a part in the hold up: an inside man aiding the bandits. Cade concluded by explaining that his pard had gone to confront Willy when the lead started to fly. Harvey, the barkeep, had more or less confirmed these events. And he even went further – being able to name the two dead men as well as the man who had fled. It had been Matthew James.

Damn fool kid, the sheriff thought. He'd warned him only yesterday after the hothead had winged that varmint in this very saloon that he was heading for a necktie party. It looked as if the kid had finally gone and done it this time. If the gunfight had happened the way King's man said it did, which seemed likely, then it was also probable that the kid had also been involved in the robbery.

'I best get a posse together,' the sheriff said. He stood up and looked Cade directly in the eye. 'You come with me. We're going to need to speak to your boss.'

'Yes, Sheriff,' Cade said, and the lawmen sensed a coldness in the man. Even if he had done his killing in self-defence he didn't seem none too bothered about it.

'Come on,' Matt said. 'I ain't telling you again. We got to vamoose.'

Cursing, Rile hopped around the room while he pulled his remaining boot on. He tucked his shirt into his pants and secured his gunbelts.

'I'm all paid up for the night here,' Rile grumbled and cast an eye at the frightened-looking girl on the bed. She was holding a sheet over herself to cover her modesty and her frightened eyes moved between the two men.

'If you don't move this'll be the last night you ever

see,' Matt snapped back. He went to the window and parted the lace curtains. There was no sign of anyone yet but he guessed it wouldn't be too long before a posse came out this way, looking for them.

'You say Clem and Hay are dead?' Rile said as he pulled his rawhide jacket on. He said it in an offhand fashion, as if it was of little consequence to him.

'Yes,' Matt said and turned from the window. 'Now come on.'

'We got to avenge their killings.'

'At the moment I'm more concerned about saving our skins.'

Rile took a lingering look around the room, his eyes coming to rest on the bed where, only moments ago, he had been cuddled up all nice and warm with the girl who called herself Sultina. He went over to her and kissed her gently on the forehead.

'Damn waste,' he said. 'But I'll be back.'

'Come on.' Matt grabbed his arm. 'Let's get some miles behind us before dark.'

TEN

It had been quite an evening, Delta thought as he stumbled towards the barn. Stumbled because he had maybe drunk too much, which wasn't really saying anything. These days he wasn't a regular drinker and the three glasses of beer he'd consumed during dinner had just about finished him off. He felt light-headed but comfortable with it. It had been some time since he'd felt this good.

In the distance an owl called out and Delta paused for a moment to look at the milky night sky; thin, wispy clouds, illuminated by the moon, drifted across the vast expanse. Standing here, looking at all this, one could truly believe that God was in his heavens.

Delta took in a deep breath of the mountain air, hoping it would clear his head somewhat, then he continued towards the barn. It was a warm night, sultry, and he was suddenly very tired.

The thought of bunking down in the barn while Etta was back in the ranch house didn't bother him none. He was, after all, at this precise time closer to her than he had been for many a year. And that in itself was more than he felt he deserved.

Delta went into the barn and threw the blankets on to a pile of straw to the left of the doorway. He guessed he would be out of any draughts and although he felt perfectly safe here, old habits died hard. If someone came in during the night, hoping to catch him unawares, he'd spring up behind them. Not that he expected anything of the kind but the years of living by his wits had made him maybe a little over-cautious. He guessed he wouldn't even curl up next to his own mother without a six-shooter beneath his pillow.

Delta had expected an intimate dinner, just himself and Etta, but the ranch foreman, Steve had also been present. He'd sat there, giving Delta looks of ill-concealed contempt. Apparently Steve had been working for Etta for over ten years, had spent more of his life with her than Delta ever had, and although Delta didn't think there was anything other than business in their relationship, it was obvious they were friendly enough and also that Steve would have liked to have taken that friendship further. Delta showing up like this sure didn't meet with the ranch foreman's approval.

Who was to blame him? Etta was still a good-looking woman and the fact that she owned so much land would make her more attractive still. She would offer not only the companionship of a good woman but also wealth and standing in the community. Land was highly sought-after these days and its call could be as alluring as that of any woman.

Delta mulled it all over as he set out his bed, making a pillow of one blanket and placing the other so he'd be able to wrap it around him. He removed his hat, boots and gunbelt but placed both guns beneath the makeshift pillow. He lay down then and closed his eyes, knowing that as soon as he found sleep he would start to dream about the man who had killed him.

These days he always seemed to dream about the man who had killed him.

He was there again but the strange thing was Delta knew he was dreaming, that none of this was real, but all the same he couldn't wake himself. No matter how hard he tried to wake, sleep held him in its clutches. He knew what was coming next, it always came, and with it Delta would feel the pain – so real in his dream and just as intense as the time it had happened for real.

Now was that time.

In his dreams it was always that time.

He knew he was going to take the pot, hard to beat a royal flush, and as he threw the cards down on the table he smiled and scooped the pile of bills and coins over the edge of the table and into his hat. He was somehow detached, as if watching his dream self go through the motions. Delta thanked the other card players, thanked them the same way in the dream as he always had, and he knew the scowls upon their faces, could paint them from memory, before they appeared here in the dream.

'You're cheating,' the weaselly-looking English gambler said. 'No one could be this lucky.'

Delta looked at the man and shook his head. It was a sad state of affairs when a man couldn't even play an honest game of cards without being slighted. He knew he had suitable provocation to make a play but he also knew he would beat the man, and he saw no reason to kill him. He had done more than enough killing in his time.

'I don't cheat,' Delta said and then smiled to ease some of the tension. 'Well hardly ever.'

'Why, you scoundrel,' Weasel-face said and stood up, going for his gun, but before he had cleared leather he was looking down the barrel of Delta's polished Colt. It had been an incredibly fast draw, even more incredible given that Delta held his hat, weighed down with coins, in his other hand.

'I don't cheat,' Delta repeated and looked at the other men around the card-table, daring any of them to contradict him, but no one did. Weasel-face decided to sit down and keep his hands visible, on the table.

'I suppose I've been called much worse than a scoundrel.' Delta holstered his gun and transferred the money from his hat into his pockets. And now the real Delta stirred in his sleep as he watched the dream Delta turn from the table and walk out of the saloon.

Don't turn your back, Delta tried to warn his dream self. Don't turn at all, back out of the saloon, Weasel-face ain't happy and in a moment he's going to put a couple of slugs in your back.

Only dreams didn't work like that and Delta was forced once again to relive the time Weasel-face had killed him.

And now the dream Delta walked towards the batwings, took those final few steps before Weasel-face killed him. In his dreams he had taken those steps a thousand times, taken those bullets too.

Here they come.

Dream Delta is in mid-step.

The real Delta turns in his sleep.

There is sweat on his brow, it spins off into the air as his head thrashes wildly back and forth, but still he doesn't wake.

And now dream Delta does a strange thing.

One moment he is walking in a steady fashion, nearing the exit and the next he arches his back and is then propelled forward as two slugs rape his flesh.

He feels the red-hot pain in his back and is spun around; then another slug enters just below his collarbone.

He hits the floor hard and through bloodshot eyes sees Weasel-face staring open-mouthed, a smoking Colt in his hand. He tries to move but can't. He fully expects to die at any moment. It becomes difficult to breathe and the pain is all-consuming. All he can do is lie there while Weasel-face comes and stands over him. Like an injured animal waiting to be put out of its misery he looks on in wild-eyed terror.

'You are a liar and a cheat,' Weasel-face says. 'And now you are a dead liar and cheat.' He turns back to the other card players, then bends and starts scooping up the fallen money into his own hat. He takes no more notice of the man lying on the floor beside him. He whistles cheerfully as he collects the last of the coins and drops them into his hat.

Delta says nothing, is incapable of speech. He feels himself slipping away into blackness as the image of Weasel-face is etched deep into his memory.

ELEVEN

Delta's eyes snapped open, a silent scream resting upon his lips.

He lay there staring into the darkness of the barn while he waited for the after-images of the dream to vanish from his mind. Soon he fell back asleep and mercifully this time the dream didn't return.

He slept, as always, not knowing whether he would ever wake up.

Delta heard the footsteps coming towards the barn. He cursed beneath his breath. He couldn't move, the paralysis had returned to his left side and it was even worse than usual. Whereas in the past it had been largely confined to his upper body, now it was total.

The doctor had explained all this to him. Both of the slugs Weasel-face had put in his back had been removed but one, the one that took him from the front, was lodged in such a position, somewhere between his spine and heart – perilously close to the heart in fact, that removal was not possible, at least, not without killing the patient. The superior-mediastinum area was the most likely place for the bullet, the doctor had explained, but even that was speculation as there was no way of probing to find its exact position. And so the bullet would have to stay where it was. There might have been some surgeons back East who would attempt such an operation, but even then, with the best hands in the business, the operation would be considered extremely risky. At first the doctor had expected infection to set in but, remarkably, it had never come and Delta had healed from the wounds. However there was no doubt that the bullet would eventually prove fatal; likely it would provoke a massive heart attack as the pressured arteries around the slug hardened and closed, but for now Delta lived.

If you could call it that.

Each day he was aware of the death sentence hanging over him and each night he didn't know whether he'd wake again come dawn; indeed sometimes he wished he wouldn't wake, that he would go in his sleep. A man couldn't walk around indefinitely carrying a chunk of lead inside him. Was there any point in delaying the inevitable?

Delta took deep rhythmic breaths, willing feeling to return. There was a slight twinge in his neck and he found he could move his head back and forth, but other than that his entire left side was dead. And now he heard Etta calling him, her voice growing clearer as she neared the barn.

He didn't want her to see him like this. Using his

right hand he managed to push himself up until he could reach the wall of the stall and use that to pull himself upright. It hurt to move, though, and he felt that bullet shift. He heartbeat seemed to jump, something he'd never felt before, like a thud within his chest; and he fully expected to die there and then, but he went on living. He gritted his teeth against the pain in his chest and managed to turn and push his back against the wall, using it to keep upright.

'There you are,' Etta said, as she entered the barn. 'It's after nine. You've slept a bunch.'

Delta nodded but didn't speak. He didn't want to risk it and have his words come out slurred, as if he were drunk.

For a moment a frown crossed Etta's face and she stared at him, maybe noticing the awkward way in which he stood, as if only the wall was holding him up.

'Are you OK?' she asked.

'Sure,' Delta managed. He felt a familiar tingling sensation in his entire left side and he was thankful that the feeling was starting to return, but with it came a cruel agony. The tingling ravaged his flesh, felt as if there were scores of carnivorous ants scuttling beneath the flesh.

'Are you coming to the house for breakfast?'

Delta nodded.

'Well, come on.'

'You go on,' Delta said. 'I have to, er. . . .'

Again Etta frowned but then she smiled.

'Well, be quick,' she said. 'We only serve the once.'

'Sure,' Delta said and again gritted his teeth. It was all he could do to stop his pain showing in his face.

Etta didn't seem at all convinced and she probed him with her eyes. She took a step closer towards him but then stopped. Concern crossed her face.

'Delta, what's wrong with you?'

'Nothing,' Delta said and he took a step towards her, taking a chance that his left leg would support him. He was thankful that it did, though the left arm still hung limply at his side. 'I just slept awkward, got some aches and pains. A little cramp I guess.'

'None of us is getting any younger,' Etta pointed out with a smile.

'Guess not,' Delta managed and, despite the roaring agony that travelled up and down his left side, he smiled.

'Maybe you are getting too old for bedding down in barns or beneath the skies.'

'I sure am that.'

'You coming for breakfast, then?'

'I'll get washed up and be right over.'

'Well, hurry,' Etta said again and this time she turned on her heels and left Delta alone.

They had ridden for most of the night, only resting the horses for an hour or two before setting off again at dawn. Matt knew they would have to stop soon – Rile's horse didn't look like it could continue much further and Matt's own mount was starting to sag.

'I think we've lost them,' Matt said.

Throughout the night the posse had been keeping

up their pursuit, but there had been no sign of them for some time and Matt guessed they would have stopped to rest their own horses. Sooner or later they'd start off again and he wanted to get much distance covered before they did. Indian Bob would be tracking for them, since Sheriff Masters was good friends with the half-breed, and it was said the old Indian could track a raindrop in a storm.

'There.' Rile pointed ahead to where the landscape started to climb towards the mountain range known as the High Lonesomes. 'We'll stop there.'

Matt nodded. Rile was right. If they stopped up ahead at the foot of the hills they would have a pretty good view if the posse approached and would be able to flee up into the hills and the mountains beyond. There was plenty of water and game in the mountains.

'Where are we going, in any case?' Rile asked.

'Beats me,' Matt replied, having to shout to be heard over the roar of the horses tearing up the now soft ground. Thus far the only desire had been to escape the posse and no long-term plan had been thought up. Everything had happened so quickly; if there was a plan, it was simply to get away from the neck-stretching crew they had in pursuit.

They would work out everything else later.

TWELVE

The breakfast had been just what Delta had needed and he ate his fill, having second helpings of the succulent bacon and then mopping his plate clean with a thick wedge of bread. Throughout the meal Steve had sat at the table, a scowl upon his face; he made no attempt to hide the resentment he so obviously felt at Delta's presence.

Again Delta wondered if there had ever been anything romantic between Etta and Steve, but once again he decided it was none of his damn business. All the same he felt a little bothered by the possibility that there might have been.

Etta was a handsome woman and when he'd turned his back on her all those years ago he'd pretty much given up any rights to her. He had to remember that, but now, all these years later, it seemed a damn fool thing to have done.

That there was something of a relationship between the ranch foreman and Etta, Delta was certain; all the other ranch hands ate at the chuck table in the bunkhouse but good old Steve was very much a part of the furnishings around the place. He treated the ranch house as home and was confident enough in his position not to bother hiding the fact that he was eager for Delta to move on and was suspicious of his motives for being here. And in truth, Delta had to admit, he didn't blame the man for it. Since Weasel-face had killed him, Delta had become painfully aware of what a selfish man he had been.

It was much too late to start making amends now.

All the same Delta was pleased when Steve left the table, mumbling something about having several hours of solid toil ahead. A statement that was plainly intended to imply that Delta didn't. The ranch foreman seemed to consider Delta little more than a saddle tramp, which, Delta supposed, was not too far from the truth.

Etta poured Delta another coffee and frowned when she heard Steve slam the door on his way out. She started to clear the breakfast dishes.

'Let me help you.' Delta stood and winced a little at the ache in his chest.

'You doing a woman's chores!' Etta teased.

'I can sure help wash a few dishes.'

'Without breaking them?'

Delta grinned and drained his coffee. He reached across the table and grabbed Steve's dish, then balanced his own upon it. He toppled them so that one of the dishes fell but before it could hit the floor he grabbed it with his free hand.

'Sure can,' he said with a grin. 'Lead me to the hot water.'

Etta laughed and picked up the rest of the dishes.

'Follow me,' she said and grinned over her shoulder as she went through to the kitchen.

Standing there, side by side at the sink, Etta washed while Delta wiped. Delta couldn't help but think that this could have been the way his life had gone if he hadn't made the choice to turn his back on it a lifetime ago. Here and now he was certain that that choice had been the wrong one. Etta seemed to have a pretty fine life and his life, or at least that which was left to him, was anything but fine.

When they had finished Etta took the towel from Delta and hung it on the line behind the stove. She rubbed her hands on her apron and looked at Delta.

'What plans you got for today?' she asked.

'Maybe take a look around,' Delta said. 'I was hoping you'd ride out with me. Visit a few memories.'

'Sure. I'd like that.'

'Maybe even take a picnic. We used to do that a lot.'

'That would be fine.'

'Good,' Delta said and smiled.

'I've got a cold ham we could use and there's some freshly baked biscuits.'

Delta winced slightly at a twinge in his side and he hoped it wouldn't prove to be the harbinger of another bout of paralysis. It was happening more and more frequently of late.

'That would be fine and dandy,' Delta said.

'I'll let Steve know we're going. You saddle up the horses and I can throw the lunch together.'

'Sure thing,' Delta answered. He followed her out of the ranch house and into the pale morning sunshine.

Steve was nowhere to be seen. Etta asked one of the ranch hands as to his whereabouts and was told he was up in the north enclosure, overseeing the branding of a bunch of horses they had recently purchased. Etta was just about to send one of the ranch hands to fetch the foreman when she saw several riders approaching from the rise above them.

Delta stood besides Etta as they watched the riders approach. They were taking the regular route down the hill, sticking firmly to the track, and as they approached Etta recognized the sheriff at the front of the procession.

'Jake,' she said, more to herself than Delta. She kept her eyes trained on the sheriff and the other men as they reached the flat lands and picked up their speed as they rode towards them.

'Sheriff Masters,' Delta said, recognizing the lawman he had faced in town a couple of days ago. It seemed like a lifetime had passed since then.

Etta swung on her feet to face Delta.

'You know Jake Masters?' she asked.

'That the sheriff's name?'

'Yes. Sheriff Jake Masters. He's been the law around here for the best part of ten years.'

'I met him in Hayes,' Delta said. 'He advised me to

leave town. Said they don't take to strangers.'

'It was you who made yourself a stranger in these parts,' Etta said accusingly, and waved as the sheriff and the posse entered the main enclosure. The sheriff dismounted and told the rest of the men to hang back while he walked over to Etta and Delta.

'Howdy,' the sheriff said and tipped his hat to Etta. He gave Delta a suspicious glance. 'Surprised to see you again, stranger.'

'I left town,' Delta said. 'You never said anything about leaving the territory.'

The sheriff frowned, then turned to Etta. 'You know this man?'

Etta looked at Delta for several moments before answering.

'I used to know him,' she said enigmatically, then she shrugged her shoulders when the sheriff gave her a puzzled look. 'What brings you out here, Jake?' she asked before anything further could be said.

'Is it OK to talk in front of him?' The sheriff pointed to Delta. The lawman regarded him the way a man might a tainted water hole.

'Sure. Now what is it, Jake?'

'It's the boy,' the sheriff said and Delta noticed the look upon Etta's face. It was pure blind panic he saw there.

'Matt?' Etta cast a glance at Delta that the man didn't truly understand.

The sheriff nodded.

'He's finally gone and done it,' he said. 'Got himself into a heap of trouble this time. That's what the posse's for. We were on his tail for most of the night but we lost him and I figured he might have come back here.'

'I've not seen Matt in a couple of weeks,' Etta said. 'You know what he's like. Always had wanderlust, that boy. Why, the last time he was here was' – she paused, searching her memory – 'a week last Tuesday, I think.'

Matt? Delta looked questions first at Etta and then at the sheriff.

'The kid from the saloon?' he asked of the sheriff.

The sheriff nodded. 'That would be Matt, yes.'

Etta grabbed Delta's arm.

'You've met Matt?'

'I guess so,' Delta said. 'We almost had a gunfight. The sheriff here can tell you.'

Matt? What was happening here? What had the kid done? And what was he to Etta?

'Why is this kid so all-fired important?' Delta asked.

'He's my son,' Etta said, then looked deep into Delta's eyes. She didn't have to say any more, it was all there in her gaze and Delta read it clearly. All the same, she said it: 'Our son.'

THIRTEEN

Matt spun the cylinder of the Colt Navy, satisfied with the smooth motion, then returned the weapon to its holster. He spat into the fire and turned suddenly, his hand hovering over the Colt when he heard movement behind him.

'You getting jumpy,' Rile said with a grin. He was carrying a large jackrabbit over his shoulder and he threw it beside the fire. 'Figured we could cook this up before we move out.'

Matt stood up and glanced down at the rabbit, a particularly large specimen that looked to have some meat on it.

'You shot it,' he said. 'You can cook it. I'm going to see if there's any sign of that posse.'

Rile lifted the rabbit and, using his knife, he disembowelled it, allowing the offal to slop to the ground. The critters hereabouts would take care of the gory slop as soon as the men moved on.

'We lost them ways back,' Rile said and removed the rabbit's head. He tossed it on to the fire. The eyes seemed to gaze accusingly at him from the flames.

'Maybe. But all the same I think I'll take me a climb and a look-see.'

'Suit yourself.' Using the knife Rile skilfully brought the rabbit's skin back from the neckline and peeled it from the flesh like the skin of a fruit. He tossed it aside.

'Save me some of that there rabbit,' Matt said. He watched Rile as he brushed the dust from the rabbit's carcass and then spilt some water from the canteen over it. 'It's sure going to taste good. My stomach thinks my throat's been slit.'

Rile selected a spit from the stack of wood besides the fire and poked it up through the rabbit. He placed it over the fire, balancing one end on a rock, then wiped his hands down the front of his Levis.

'Sure thing,' he said. 'There's enough here for four men.'

Matt nodded, then walked towards the hill.

Matt climbed the hill, looking for a vantage point that would allow him to see for miles around. They had to work out their plan of action. King's money was hidden away and they would need that, every single cent, if they were going to embark on a life on the lam.

Not that they had any choice in the matter. After the shoot-out in the Double Diamond it wasn't only a robbery charge they had to face. It had been Hayloft who had drawn first and ignited the gunfight. In the exchange both Hayloft and Clement had lost their lives, as well as one of King's men. Matt figured he could maybe face the hangman for his part in all this. The only option open to them looked to be a life spent trying to stay one step ahead of the law and Matt was starting to have serious doubts about the way he'd been living his life just lately. It had seemed an exciting prospect to steal from Maxwell King. After all, he wasn't well-liked and had forced landowners to sell to him for a fraction of the true worth of their spreads. King had deserved to be robbed, but Matt's thinking hadn't gone any further than that. The robbery had been all he had considered and not what could possibly happen afterwards.

It bothered him the way things had played out.

It was mighty strange the way King's man had lunged at Willy like that, as if trying to silence him in some way. But none of that made any sense to Matt and there were many more questions he couldn't answer.

Why hadn't the robbery been reported?

Was that why King's man had attacked Willy?

Had he thought the robbery was an inside job and Willy was involved?

It all made no sense. Surely directly following the robbery Willy and the driver would have returned to King and told him what had happened: that the monthly pay-run had been snatched. Then the sheriff would have been alerted and a posse formed. But the gang wouldn't be found because they would already be back in town, going about life in the same old way until things cooled down. Only that was not the way it had played out and for the life of him Matt couldn't figure out why King hadn't been screaming blue murder over the robbery.

Maxwell King hadn't really slept last night and he was in an even fouler mood than usual. Not only was he fuming that someone had had the sheer audacity to steal from him, but the fact that Willy had managed to slip away again was constantly gnawing at his mind.

The news of the robbery was out now and if the sheriff got to Willy before they did and discovered that Clift had not been shot in the hold-up, then things could get mighty tricky around here. King had power and influence in the town but all the same Sheriff Masters was not a man to be messed around with. The lawman couldn't be bought or controlled, as could most people. King knew that, having dropped subtle hints to the lawman in the past: the suggestion of regular payments to supplement the meagre wage he got from the town, but all that had achieved was a stony look from the sheriff. Money mattered little to the lawman and King knew that any man not governed by money could be unpredictable.

King buckled his gunbelt on and slipped into his riding-jacket. He crossed the room and examined himself before the full-sized mirror. He liked to look good, did Mr King, no matter where he was going or what he intended to do.

'How many men do you think we need?' King asked. He adjusted his necktie, then turned from the mirror and lit himself a cigar.

'I figure no more than six good men,' Cade said.

'We can run the kid down with six good men.'

'Six men for one kid?'

'Well, er, yes,' Cade said. 'Now that the law's involved and things have gone all complicated we don't want to take any chances on the kid getting the slip on us. Six men should do it. When we find him, we'll surround him and cut off any avenue of escape.'

'Of course,' King said thoughtfully. He mumbled rather than spoke. 'Clift said there had been five bandits. The kid could have an accomplice with him. There could be two of them.'

Cade shrugged his shoulders.

'Six men should still do the job,' he said.

King paced the room, pungent cigar smoke billowing out behind him. He clasped his hands behind his back and sucked hard on the cigar. After a moment he turned on his heel and removed the cigar from between his teeth. He spat out a shred of tobacco that had stuck to his lower lip, replaced the cigar into his mouth, then ran a hand through his hair.

'And we need to find Willy pretty quickly,' he said.

'Couple of the boys are out looking for him now,' Cade said. 'They'll find the drunken old coot.'

'Like you and Miller did, you mean?' King glared at the other man.

'It was you who killed Clift,' Cade pointed out, and wished he hadn't when he saw the sudden blaze in King's eyes. He swallowed audibly, thinking that he had maybe gone a step too far.

'To use the American vernacular,' King said, his

voice calm and even, his tone matter of fact. 'I call the shots around here. I will shoot whom I want whenever I want and what I say goes. No argument, no dissenting voices.'

'Yes sir, Mr King.' Cade didn't like to see King like this. He had seen him like it so many times before and he knew how nasty the man could be. More than nasty: the Englishman could be insanely evil.

'The sheriff and his posse could not have found him,' King said. 'If they had word would have reached us by now.'

Cade shrugged his shoulders.

It was true King had men in town loyal to him and they had been told to bring word the moment the posse returned. The fact that no word had come meant that there was nothing to report. There was no doubt that King would be informed the moment something happened.

'We'll ride out to the James place,' King said after a short silence.

'You think the kid'll return there?'

'Home is where the heart is.' King smiled and clasped the cigar between his teeth. 'And besides, I'd like to know how Etta is going to defend that urchin of hers this time.'

FOURTEEN

Delta didn't know what to think. He had a son, a full-grown boy. The boy was almost twenty-one, which meant that Etta must have been in the early weeks of the pregnancy when he'd ridden out all those years ago.

Why hadn't she said?

Had she even known?

It was a hell of a way for a man to find out he had blood kin he'd previously known nothing about. If there had been any hopes of getting to know the boy in the time left to Delta they had been dashed by the fact that the boy, his son, was on the lam, running from the law with charges of robbery and murder hanging over his head. Talk about bitter-sweet, first he finds out he has a son and then he is told that son is a cold-blooded killer and bandit. Like father like son, he thought cynically but then corrected himself. He might have had many failings himself but cold-blooded killing was not one of them.

The sheriff had taken Etta's news in his stride and

had just finished telling the story. Matt and his accomplices had robbed Mr King's wagon, stealing a sizeable sum. During the robbery they had shot the wagon driver, one Clift Henderson, who had made it back to King's ranch before passing over from his wounds. Later Matt and two other men, assumed to be those who had aided him in robbing the wagon, had got into a gunfight in the Double Diamond. The fight had resulted in the deaths of both of Matt's accomplices and one of King's men. Matt escaped and it was thought he had joined up with another man, since the posse had picked up the tracks of two riders, before fleeing. That was pretty much how it stood and the sheriff was certain that King would place a large ransom on Matt's head. Given that Matt was a killer, the terms would most likely be dead or alive with the emphasis on the former.

'My son,' Delta said dreamingly, as if the news was only now sinking in. In truth he thought it would be quite some time before it truly sank in. He felt as if he had been struck in the stomach, kicked in the face and then some. It was all too much to take in and he felt himself reeling with confusion. 'My son,' he repeated.

Etta looked at him and the sadness in her eyes touched his.

'You left,' she said. 'I'd only then found out I was with child. I was going to tell you the very morning you upped sticks and rode out. All I knew was that I was left alone and I was with child.'

'I didn't know,' Delta said, as if it were an excuse for the bad decisions he had made.

'No.' Etta shook her head. 'You didn't know.'

Steve had joined them mid-way through the sheriff's speech and he stood there, awkwardly kicking his feet in the dirt. He seemed more taken aback by the news that Matt was Delta's son than anyone else. He just stood there, shaking his head and mumbling beneath his breath.

'No one forced me to go,' Delta said. 'If I had have known—'

'You'd what?' Etta cut in. 'You would have stayed? Is that what you're saying?'

Delta looked away from her.

'I don't rightly know,' he said and left it at that.

'Well,' the sheriff said, playing the diplomat. 'I thought you folks had the right to know. You realize if he comes around here you'll have to notify me? I just hope we can find him before he gets in any more gunfights. The longer this goes on the more certain it becomes he'll face the noose.'

'Yes.' Etta took a step closer to the sheriff and clasped his hands in her own. 'Thank you, Jake.'

The sheriff blushed. 'That's OK.'

'Don't let anyone hurt him, Sheriff.'

'You have my word.' The sheriff glanced between Steve and Delta, as if beseeching one or the other to comfort this woman. 'I'll make sure Matt gets a fair trial. Whatever happens then,' he paused, searching for the right words, 'well, I guess it's in the hands of the Almighty.'

'Are you sure?' Etta asked. Steve pulled her away from the sheriff when she grabbed his shirtfront. 'Are you sure Matt did these things?'

The sheriff didn't look Etta in the eye when he answered; instead he cast his eyes down to the ground and mumbled: 'I'm sure.'

With that the sheriff walked back to his horse and mounted up. He took one last look at Etta and the two men, then set off back to town, the posse following behind.

The sheriff's dust cloud was all but invisible before any of them spoke. Steve was still holding the sobbing Etta and Delta stood besides them, head bowed. It was Delta who spoke, but he kept his head down, real tears filling his eyes.

'I'm going after the boy,' He said.

'I'm coming with you.' Steve let go of Etta and turned to face Delta.

'I prefer to go alone.'

'I don't rightly care what your prefer,' Steve said. 'You may be Matt's pa, but I've known that boy since he was five years old. I've been more of a pa to him than you ever could be.'

'That's as maybe,' Delta said, fighting the wave of anger Steve's words provoked within him. 'But I travel faster alone.'

'I know this country,' Steve said. 'You're nothing more than a stranger.'

Delta looked Steve in the eyes and for a moment it seemed his anger would get the better of him. But then he nodded, said: 'I guess I am that.'

'I'm coming and that's the end of it,' Steve snapped, putting a period on the conversation.

'Suit yourself.' Delta started towards the stables. He didn't look in Etta's direction and he turned his back on her sobs. He was still stunned by the morning's events and, just at that moment, he didn't know what he'd say to her.

What the hell could he say to her?

'It'll be risky getting to the money,' Matt pointed out. 'They're going to be looking for us. It's way too risky.'

'We're going to need that money,' Rile said. 'If we're going to get far enough away to stop looking over our shoulders we're going to need that money. Why, if we leave the money then none of this makes any sense. It'll mean that Hay and Clem died for nothing.'

Matt nodded. He knew his friend was right but all the same going back for the money now seemed like pushing their luck just that little too much. The money was hidden fairly close to town, within two miles of its boundaries and Matt didn't think it would ever truly be without risk to return for it.

'Maybe a few days.' Matt spat into the fire. They were clean out of tobacco and at that moment he would have given anything for a smoke.

'If the posse figures we ain't got King's money with us, that we would stash it somewhere,' Rile said, 'then they'd be expecting us to let the dust settle before collecting it. The last thing they'd expect is for us to head towards town now. The element of surprise means now may be the safest time of all to return.'

Matt looked at Rile and had to admit that he had a very good point. He may have been a hothead and prone to random acts of madness but he was sure talking a lot of sense at the moment. If they could slip by the posse, then returning for the money at once would probably be safer than waiting a day, a week, or a month even.

'We could ride up into the High Lonesomes,' Rile said. 'Approach town from the east and go right around the posse.'

The High Lonesomes stretched clean across the territory but taking that route would take them through King's land. Matt figured that King would have his own trigger-happy men out looking for them but maybe the last place the posse would look was on King's own property.

'It's a risk,' Matt repeated.

'We need that money,' Rile reminded him. 'This is no time to play chicken.'

Matt's gaze strengthened. He stood up and stared down at Rile, looking him straight in the eye.

'I already told you, I ain't no chicken,' he said.

'Good.' Rile stood up and brushed himself down. He kicked dirt over the fire and picked up his rifle. 'Then that's settled. Let's get going.' He grabbed his saddle blanket from the ground and tossed it over his horse. 'We set out straight away and ride through the night, and I reckon we'll have the money by dawn.'

Matt watched Rile mount up, then shook his head. He couldn't help the feeling that Rile had just put one over on him.

FIFTEEN

'Tell me about this King fella,' Delta said and slowed his horse to a trot, keeping parallel to Steve. He took a plug of chewing tobacco from his shirt pocket and bit off a portion.

Steve shifted in his saddle, using the saddle horn for support while he wiggled his aching rump. 'Not much to tell really,' he said. 'I've only ever seen him around town a bunch of times, just to say hello to but nothing else. He's been out to the ranch a few times, trying to take advantage of Etta in one deal or another.'

'Etta has dealings with King?'

'No.' Again Steve shifted in the saddle. 'I think King assumed Etta, a woman alone and all that, would be a pushover. He's tried to buy land from her or sell her some of his own. But Etta's not a foolish woman and as soon as King savvied to that he pretty much left us alone.'

'King own a lot of land?'

'His spread's huge,' Steve said. 'The biggest

around these parts.'

'What's his thing – cattle, horses?'

Steve shrugged his shoulders. 'King only arrived in Hayes a couple of years back, clutching the deeds to the old Hale ranch, which he claimed to have won in a poker game. Since then he's cheated a lot of folk and bought up land like it was going out of style. Most of the land he owns is pretty much useless for anything but, well, who knows how a snake like that thinks?'

'An empire-builder.'

'A som-bitch is what he is,' Steve said, giving his considered evaluation. 'He's a strange looking guy, all English charm but as black-hearted as they come. A few times he's had trouble with town people or other landowners but they kind of move in and are never really seen again. Yep, King's a som-bitch, sure enough.'

Delta, who had once known an Englishman, indeed had been killed by that Englishman, nodded, said: 'They usually are.' Weasel-face was certainly a cold-hearted bastard.

They rode on for some time in silence. Steve, who knew the country and had a good idea where Matt would have headed, led the way with Delta hanging back, lost in his own thoughts. He wanted to ask Steve about Matt but he felt awkward, as if by being here he was intruding on Steve's own relationship with Etta and the boy. And maybe he was – he still hadn't established just what that relationship was. Eventually Steve broke the silence, speaking of Matt, and Delta felt a twinge deep inside him at the mention of the boy's name.

'Matt's always been a bit wild,' Steve said. 'But I don't cotton to him turning out a killer.'

Delta thought back to when he had squared up to the kid in the saloon. The kid could have killed that man he'd been arguing with back then but instead he'd merely winged the varmint. If he were a killer then it would be unlikely he'd be cold-blooded. Delta had known plenty of men who had enjoyed killing and not one of them would have left it at winging the man in the saloon. They would have laughed at his pain as he rolled about in the sawdust and then put one between his eyes, though probably not before putting a few slugs elsewhere to cause maximum pain.

'The sheriff seemed pretty certain,' Delta pointed out.

'Yeah, well.' Steve removed his bandanna and used it to mop his forehead. 'I need more facts before I condemn the boy.'

There was obviously affection felt for the boy by the ranch foreman, which bothered Delta somewhat since his own feelings were somewhat undefined. He may have been the kid's pa but that meant nothing: they were strangers, hadn't even known each other when they'd met in the saloon.

'This sure is a hell of a way for a man to find out he has a son,' Delta said.

Steve turned in his saddle and looked Delta directly in the eyes for a moment before speaking.

'You really think you have the right to call yourself his pa?' Steve asked. 'You weren't there when he was growing up, you never comforted the small boy when he was scared of the boogie-man, nor did you guide him when he needed guidance.'

Delta's eyes narrowed and he had to bite back the anger the foreman's words provoked. He felt a twinge in his side and his left arm started to go numb. He gripped the reins more tightly with his good hand and tried to keep the pain from registering in his face.

'Guess I deserve that,' he managed, then lowered his head as he rode on.

Steve shook his own head. There was something bothering him about the other man but he was not sure what it was. He was a strange one, sure enough, and from the sound of it had lived the life of a drifter, never throwing down roots. He supposed it couldn't have been easy for Delta to discover he had a son. Despite his distrust he felt some sympathy for the man.

'Let's go find the boy,' Steve said and spurred his horse into a gallop.

Delta did likewise, though his entire upper left side was paralysed. He held the reins tightly with his right hand and practised his breathing exercises while he waited for the paralysis to pass.

Hoped it would pass.

Ironic, that he so wanted to live.

That he had come here to die and yet he had found a reason to live.

He had long accepted the fact that he was living on borrowed time and each time the paralysis, or the fevers, or the drunken feelings returned he had hoped it would be the time that Weasel-face's bullet finally did its business. But he always recovered, kept on breathing, kept on living. It was as if he was too stubborn to die.

Now, though, he was thankful that he had thus far escaped the inevitable. He had a son and that son needed his help. Though what he could do exactly was beyond him; but he had to try.

He held on more tightly to the reins with his good hand, ignoring the paralysis, concentrating his mind on the kid.

If there was one thing Maxwell King hated about life in the New World, and that was how he referred to and thought of it: basically a uppity colony even if they had won their so called independence long before he was even born, it was the amount of riding involved to get anywhere. He was never comfortable in the saddle, was suited to neither the English nor the Western style of riding, and a ride of more than a couple of miles was apt to leave him even more belligerent than usual.

Cade rode besides his boss and behind them followed four other riders. They were all armed to the teeth, and retrieving the stolen money was secondary to the killing they had in mind. Each of them knew that when they had tracked down the kid, as soon as King had the money back he would be shot down like a mangy dog. King would say that the killing was justified, that it would send a message out to anyone else loco enough to try stealing from Maxwell King. He was a big man in these parts and had a reputation to keep. And besides that there was the fact that the kid, if taken to jail, would deny shooting Clift. It was doubtful that anyone would believe him but it could still complicate things, especially with Willy gone to ground.

'She ain't gonna tell us even if the kid is here,' Cade said. They had reached the boundaries of the Big J. Ahead of them stood the magnificent ranch house Etta James called home.

'We'll see,' King said. He scanned the ground ahead of them and could see no sign of life. 'Place looks deserted.'

'Nope.' Cade pointed towards the ranch house, to where movement could be seen. There were several figures and they all turned as one at the sound of the approaching riders.

King squinted his eyes against the sun glare. As they rode into the main enclosure he could make out Etta James; several men were scattered around her, watching their approach. King told Cade to stay with him and ordered the four other men to hang back. He knew how feisty Etta could be; he didn't want to ride in looking like a lynch mob.

'Miss James,' King said as he pulled his horse to a stop. 'How wonderful you are looking.'

'State you business and stow you bullshit,' Etta said and snatched a rifle from one of her men. She held it across her chest, her finger nestling on the trigger. She wasn't about to take any nonsense from the slimy Englishman.

King clucked his tongue upon the roof of his mouth. He cast a glance at Cade, telling him to be ready with the iron should the need arise, then he dismounted.

'I would much prefer it to be better circumstances that brought me here,' King said and brushed himself down. He tied the horse's reins to a fence post and gave Etta a slight smile. 'It's your son I'm looking for.'

'Matt's mighty popular at the moment,' Etta said.

'He robbed me, you know.'

'So I've heard,' Etta said. Then she shook her head, a slight smile on her face. 'Can't believe it's as straightforward as that, though. Not when you're involved.'

'What are you implying?' King asked.

'Nothing.' Etta looked at the four riders hanging back at the entrance to the main enclosure. She didn't like what she saw; each of them looked to be heavily armed.

'He killed one of my men in a gunfight in town,' King continued. 'And either he or one of his partners was responsible for the wounds sustained by the stage driver. Wounds that proved fatal.'

'I've heard that too.'

King glanced back at Cade and raised his eyebrows. He turned back to Etta and his eyes scanned the cowboys gathered around her. They were all wearing sidearms and several of them also carried rifles.

'You do realize your son will have to answer for his crimes?' King said eventually.

Etta nodded. 'My son will answer for any crimes he committed, but in a court of law and not to a lynch mob.'

'Of course.' King smiled. 'I wouldn't want it any other way. Why, my own great country is built on law and order and I can see this one aspires to such. No, I sure enough wouldn't want it any other way.'

'You wouldn't get it any other way.'

King laughed at that. He liked strong independent women and usually treated it as a challenge to bend them to his will. Etta, he knew from past experience, was very much her own woman and didn't need a man to fight her battles for her. She was strong and resourceful and if things had been different King would have liked to take her for his own.

'Has he been here?' King asked presently.

'Who?'

'That son of yours. Who else?'

'No.' Etta shook her head. 'I've not seen him. Not that I'd tell you in any case.'

King looked around. The kid could have been hiding anywhere – in the ranch house itself, or in one of the many outbuildings. He would have liked to push Etta aside and order his men to search the place, but to attempt to do so would surely provoke a fight. And Etta had more guns around her than he had. There odds were not favourable to the Englishman.

'Back in England,' King said, 'we use the hounds to run down a fox. That's what we're going to do here. We're going to run your boy down like the vermin he is.'

Etta raised her rifle and pointed it directly at King. Cade shifted for his own weapon but he changed his mind when several guns pointed at him. If gunfire did break out then it was likely both he and King would be the first casualties.

'You're the only vermin around here,' Etta said. 'Now get off my land before I shoot you down. And take these puppets you call a posse with you.'

King glared at Etta and then at the ranch hands around her. Each of the men held his gun pointed at either King or Cade.

'This could be considered an act of war,' King said.

'It's an act of telling you to get your sorry arse off my property.' Etta stood firm, her men beside her ready to thrown down their lives in her defence. 'I'm not telling you again. Now vamoose.'

King climbed back on his horse and exchanged a glance with Cade. He relaxed back into his saddle and took one last look at Etta James.

'You are making a grave mistake here,' King snarled. 'Hell is coming down on your boy.'

'Get going.' Etta said and fired a shot off into the air, spooking both King's and Cade's horses into a gallop. Etta laughed along with her men, but the humour failed to shift the dread she felt in her heart.

She stood there watching as King and his men rode into the distance, continuing to stand there long after her own men had returned to their business and King's men became specks on the horizon and then vanished from view entirely. Then and only then did she turn on her heel and head back towards the ranch house.

This was all such a mess and she wondered where Steve and Delta were at this precise moment. She hoped that they would catch up with her son before King's men did. It wasn't so much Matt's safety she was worried about but more the fact that he would add more dead men to his tally. That he would have more blood to answer for when he eventually faced trial.

SIXTEEN

Delta shifted so as to get more comfortable.

He stared into the fire while he drank coffee from a tin cup. Steve sat opposite, smoking a cigarette while he allowed his food to settle. Earlier Delta had shot a particularly large wild turkey and they had both eaten their fill. There was also enough of the meat left over to eat cold for breakfast.

They could have been old friends sharing a camp-fire rather than men who had known each other only days. Delta found himself warming to Steve; he seemed a good, solid man, just the sort of man needed to take care of Etta and the kid when Delta cashed in his chips. Amazing really, Delta thought, that he should mull over such considerations. He'd never been here himself to take care of the woman and boy. Indeed he'd never even known of the boy's existence until Etta had dropped that little revelation.

'We made good time today,' Steve said. He bent over the fire, refilling his cup with coffee. 'If we set out before dawn it shouldn't be too long before we pick up on Matt's tracks.'

Delta kept his gaze directed at the fire, spat, and said: 'If we're heading the right way.'

'We're going the right way.'

'I hope you're right.'

'Where else would the kid go?' Steve asked. 'He'd want to get as far away from town as possible. To the west is San Vega; he wouldn't go there and he certainly wouldn't go anywhere near town. No, I know the kid and he's heading towards the High Lonesomes. It's the only thing that makes any sense.'

'I hope you're right.'

'I know the kid,' Steve repeated.

Delta felt those words. Steve, of course, had not meant to imply anything by them, but the fact was that Delta knew nothing about the kid, his own son. And here and now, watching the flames dance into the velvet star-studded sky, Delta wondered what he was hoping to achieve. Did he think he'd be able to talk some sense into the boy, stop him from taking the owl-hoot trail that would eventually consume his life? Did he think he'd be able to tell the kid he was his father and make everything fine and dandy?

'I don't,' he said at last. 'I don't know him at all.'

Steve took the makings from his shirt pocket and made another cigarette. He lit it directly from the fire and offered Delta the coffee pot.

'Want to tell me what happened?'

Delta poured himself a fresh coffee, handed the pot back, said: 'I don't rightly know.' He sipped at the coffee and despite his usual guarded nature he found himself opening up.

'I loved Etta. I guess I still love her,' he said and looked Steve directly in the eyes. It was alien for him to talk to another man like this, a man who, when all was said and done was little more than a stranger. And yet Delta felt something of a kinship with him and he guessed that if any man could understand what he meant it was Steve.

'What drove you away?'

'I don't think I know the answer to that.' Delta used his own makings to build himself a smoke. 'You know the way a man's always looking for something he can conquer. No matter what's he's got, or maybe he just doesn't realize what he's got, but there's always that attraction of something bigger, something better. Something more. It's human nature I suppose.'

'I guess so.'

'You see, I was with Etta when she started the ranch – we started the ranch. We came here together. We were never married but folks just assumed we were, and I guess we maybe intended to one day, but it never seemed to happen. And folks took us to be married and we saw no reason to tell them otherwise.'

'You never did though?' Steve asked. 'Get married, I mean.'

'No.' Delta looked back into the past with clarity of mind such as he had never known before. 'We lived together as a married couple and planned for the future like a married couple. We were to all intents and purposes a married couple and it felt like we were married.'

'So how'd you drift apart?'

'We didn't, not exactly.'

'That makes a whole heap of sense.' Steve grinned and flicked the remains of his smoke into the fire.

'Working the ranch was hard; we were scraping by but nothing else. I heard of a silver find up north that rivalled the Comstock and I figured a few months' working a claim and we'd be able to spend the rest of our days in luxury. I just upped and went one day, having no idea that Etta was pregnant.'

'Why didn't you come back till now?'

'Things never did work out the way I thought.' Delta inhaled a lungful of smoke and allowed it to trickle out between his teeth. 'Things never did and I figured I'd maybe make money some other way before returning. I figured another month maybe, but that turned into a year. And before I knew it I was twenty years uglier and twenty years older.'

For several moments there was silence, both men lost to their own thoughts. It was Delta who spoke next.

'Tell me,' he said, clearing his throat, 'did Etta ever speak of me? I mean what did you think had happened to the kid's pa?'

'She never mentioned you in all the time I've known her,' Steve said. He looked long and hard at Delta. He added: 'I don't think she ever stopped thinking about you, though.'

That lifted Delta's spirits somewhat and he grinned awkwardly.

'When I first met Etta,' Steve continued, 'Matt was little more than a baby in arms and the ranch was nothing more than an oversized shack. No offence.'

'None taken.'

'I helped her build the place up, hired other men as the ranch and stock grew. I grew as close to Etta as it was possible to get and I think I maybe hoped something romantic would develop. But she kept our relationship one of friendship and wouldn't allow it to go anywhere else. She always kept a part of herself private and I felt that there was something between us, preventing us getting together. I guess that something was you.'

'She never mentioned me, though? Never said what happened?'

'No,' Steve shook his head. 'I asked once about Matt's pa and she just told me she never wanted to talk about it. The subject was never brought up again. You were a lucky man to have her love.'

'Don't I know it,' Delta said and he truly did know it. 'I was searching for easy money, thinking wealth was the way to happiness. And I already had everything a man could need but I didn't realize it. I've been a fool.'

'You won't get no argument from me there.'

'Is Matt a good kid?' Delta asked after a period of silence.

'He's a strong man,' Steve said. 'But he's got a wild streak in him and he rebelled against a life spent working the ranch. Right up until he was seventeen years of age he worked the ranch like he'd been born to it, but then he suddenly turned, said he wanted more excitement, that he couldn't stay in one place.'

'I can sure understand that.'

'Like father like son,' Steve said with a wry grin.

Before Delta could reply they heard the sound of riders approaching and Delta immediately sprang alert.

They both peered into the darkness, listening. There sounded to be two horses, still some way off but getting closer. They had made camp in a secluded spot, surrounded by trees, and Delta felt that whoever it was out there was so far unaware of the camp; it seemed best to keep it that way. The campfire had been kept low and its illumination wouldn't break through the tree line. Delta doubted if the smell of smoke would be detectable more than a few feet away.

'What do you think?' Delta asked.

Steve looked at him for a moment, shrugging his shoulders.

No telling who it was out there.

'Douse the fire,' Delta said. 'And let's go take a look-see.'

SEVENTEEN

Delta drove their horses deeper into the scrub and then returned to Steve. Together they lay on the ground, using a bank as natural cover, while they listened to the riders approaching.

'There's definitely two of them,' Delta said.

Steve nodded in agreement.

They both listened for a while longer. Whoever the riders were they didn't care who heard them and they were making no attempt to silence their movement. Probably a couple of cowboys heading for Hayes, Delta thought.

'I don't think they're gonna smell the campfire,' Steve said. 'A regular couple of greenhorns.'

That was also Delta's assessment. Although much of the West was now civilized and the period the dime novels called 'The Wild West' was now fading into history, there could still be danger at each and every turn. No matter what the politicians said, there were still bandits operating across the Western territories. Only a month back Delta had been told of hostile bands of Sioux raiding along the old

Bozeman trail. And yet these two unknown riders, still concealed by the darkness, were riding along as if they were the only two people in the world.

'There,' Steve whispered, pointing. 'I see them.'

The moon was high in the sky and much of its illumination was filtered out by the hills but sure enough Delta picked up the outline of the two figures. They rode side by side, chatting as they went, and although their features weren't visible he could make out that it was most definitely two men. They were riding across the flatlands and would bypass the banking behind which Delta and Steve hid.

'Heading towards town,' Steve said.

'Recognize either of them?'

'I'm not sure,' Steve said and squinted his eyes as he tried to pick out anything familiar about the figures, but they were little more than silhouettes against the night sky.

'Don't suppose it's any of our business who they are or where they're headed,' Delta said. It was always wise for a man to keep his attention on matters of his own concern. It was something of an unwritten rule between men in the West.

'Guess so,' Steve said. He was about to turn away when he noticed something about the riders. 'Sombitch,' he said, no longer bothering to keep his voice low.

'What is it?' Delta looked up, startled by Steve's manner.

'It's Matt,' Steve said. He stood and hollered to the two riders. 'It's the kid.'

*

Maxwell King pulled his blanket more tightly around him, cursing the sudden chill in the air. He gazed at the moon; trying to figure out what time it was, but then gave up and pulled the chain that held his watch out. He tilted the watch, using the moonlight to illuminate the watch face.

Almost 4.30.

It would be dawn soon.

The plan had been that he would stay with the men in the search for the kid, but during the night he had changed his mind. He just wasn't cut out for sleeping beneath the stars with the hard ground as a mattress and the rough woollen blanket and the sorry-looking campfire the only source of warmth. No, at first light he'd set off back to his spread, taking Cade with him, while the other men continued the search.

He stood up, stretching the aches out of his muscles, then made a cigarette. He struck a sulphur match against his boot heel and smiled when he saw Cade looking up at him.

'Can't sleep?' Cade asked.

'No.' King shook his head. 'I think we'd best get some coffee on.'

Cade sat up and rubbed his face in his hands. Around him the other men were starting to stir, woken by the voices.

'I'll get some wood for the fire,' he said. 'Soon feel better.'

King nodded and stood there while he thought of the way things were starting to unravel. Willy was still missing and the kid was out there somewhere, on the run with his money. It was getting very messy and there was now the real possibility that word would get out that Clift hadn't been shot in the robbery at all. The longer things went on the more likely it was that Willy would emerge and blurt out the truth to someone. King didn't want that, knew that he wouldn't be able to buy himself out of that kind of trouble. Sheriff Masters would just love to hang a murder charge on Maxwell King.

King was starting to realize that capturing the kid was not the most important thing here. It had become a far greater priority to locate and silence Willy. After all, the kid could protest that he'd not been involved in the shooting of Clift until he was blue in the face and no one would believe him, but with Willy saying pretty much the same thing it would cause the eye of suspicion to turn in King's direction.

He couldn't have that.

King had a good thing going here. For the first time in his life he was prosperous and had standing in the community among which he had made his home. He owned more land even than the Hayes Company, and they had started the goddamn town, built a community here when it was little more than a playground for the heathen savages who once populated the mountains hereabouts.

He had jeopardized everything he had worked for and built, and all in a moment of fury when he had pumped a .44 into Clift. Until that point he had been the man wronged. Yet by shooting Clift he had committed a crime far greater than larceny.

Cade returned with armfuls of wood and tossed several logs on to the fire. He bent to the fire and blew, coaxing flames from the embers and in a moment the thinner branches of wood had caught nicely.

'Soon have the coffee brewing,' Cade said and poured water into the pot from his canteen. Above them the dawn was breaking through and the sky looked magnificent in all its azure wonder.

'We'll return to the ranch,' King said. 'The others can continue to search for the kid. I think we'd be better employed hunting down Willy.'

Cade nodded but said nothing.

'We'll set off immediately following breakfast,' King said and made himself another cigarette. 'I'm getting too old for this kind of life.'

'You and me both,' Cade said and sat back beside the fire. The other men also huddled around the fire, waiting for the coffee that would wash the sleepy feeling from their bones. No one said anything about King's plans; to a man they knew that there was no use arguing with the boss. He was a stubborn man and could get extremely nasty when his words were questioned.

'When you do find the kid,' King said, addressing them all around the campfire, 'I don't want him brought back to town alive. Even if he comes peaceably I want him dead.'

No one said a word but King's words echoed around each of their minds.

EIGHTEEN

'That puts an entirely new slant on things,' Delta said. 'I'm not sure what exactly. But if you're telling the truth then it ain't as clear cut as it first seemed.'

'Then who shot the stage driver?' Matt asked.

The four of them were sitting around the fire. Delta had just finished telling Matt and Rile about the situation in town, of the claims that had been made following the gunfight in the Double Diamond. But both Matt and Rile, although admitting to the robbery, denied having anything to do with killing the driver. The worst they had done was shoot William McCord's hat from his head, and when they had left with the proceeds of their robbery Clift was still very much alive. As for Willy, well, he ran off into the scrub and neither of them were too sure where he'd gone from there. But during the robbery only one shot had been fired and all that had done was to kill Willy's hat.

'From the way you tell it,' Delta said at last, 'it makes some kind of sense.'

'How?' Matt looked at the man and couldn't help feeling he was missing something. The man had told him that he was an old friend of his mother's but there was definitely something going on between the man and Steve.

Some secret between them.

Matt could sense it.

'King's man moving suddenly and pistol whipping this Willy,' Delta said. He looked his son squarely in the eyes. He so wanted to tell him that he was his father, blurt it out here and now, but he resisted the urge. 'Maybe he was making sure he silenced him before something was blurted out.'

'Like what really happened to the driver?' Matt asked.

Delta nodded. Matt was a smart kid, even if the robbery had been strictly amateur, a clumsy snatch and grab; he was following the train of thought perfectly, which gave Delta an absurd feeling of pride. This boy was very much his son; he could feel it now and he felt in a strange way that deep down he had known it that first time he had seen him in the saloon.

'If we can prove you didn't kill the driver,' Steve put in, addressing Matt directly, 'then you won't be facing a rope for your part in the robbery. And if King was responsible for the killing and we can prove that then you may get away without any charges.'

'What about the money?' Rile put in.

'Is it important?' Delta asked. 'Is that the most important thing?'

'Damn right it's important,' Rile snapped.

Matt was in agreement with his partner. 'We ain't giving the money back.'

'You want to live the life of an outlaw?' Delta asked. 'Is that what you want? A life like that can only end one way and that's with you dead. Believe me, I've known that kind of life.'

Matt looked at Delta, astonished by the outburst. The man might be an old friend of his mother, but the man's concern seemed way over the top. It seemed as if the man felt he had some sort of responsibility here.

'You ain't dead,' Matt pointed out.

'Ain't I?' Delta snapped back, letting his words hang in the air. He felt like telling them of the bullet he carried inside him but he said nothing. There was nothing that could be said and when his time came he'd face it with a grin, but for now he lived and he could at last see a reason for his being here, a purpose in each borrowed breath, and that was to ensure that this kid, his son, didn't throw his life away before it had really begun.

'He's right, Matt,' Steve said. He looked at Delta for a moment. 'We've got to take you back into town, square things up with the sheriff and return the money. That may be enough.'

'Screw that.' Rile hit the ground with his hat in frustration. 'If you think I'm going to give myself up you're just loco.'

'It would be loco to run,' Delta said. 'Run from a killing you didn't do. Now that's loco.'

'So what?' Matt grinned. 'We go tell the sheriff we didn't kill the wagon driver, give the money back and that'll be it? They'll tell us we've been bad boys and leave it at that?'

Silence fell for a moment while each of them contemplated Matt's mostly valid point. A wave of hopelessness seemed to descend upon the camp, but then Delta broke the mood.

'You can't just hand yourselves in,' he said. 'I can see that, but if we can prove you didn't kill the driver then we can maybe cast doubt on the whole thing. It's King who said you robbed the wagon and killed the driver, but if we can prove the killing weren't down to you two then maybe we can say there weren't no robbery either.'

'But who did kill the driver?' Matt asked.

'Likely be King himself or someone very close to him,' Delta said.

'I don't follow your figuring.' This time it was Steve who spoke.

'The way the sheriff told it,' Delta said, 'it was the driver who told him Matt's gang did the robbery. If King's lying there then it stands to reason he was in some way responsible for the shooting of the driver.'

'Why would King shoot his own man?' Again it was Steve.

'Who knows why men do such things?' Delta said. 'I don't know the man but thinking about it logically I'd say he shot him in fury after learning of the robbery. Maybe the driver did tell King about Matt's gang doing the robbery but I'd bet my life he weren't shot up none.'

'Makes sense.' Steve had to agree.

Matt looked at Delta. 'Willy,' he said.

'Willy?' Delta looked at the kid and again he had to resist the very real urge to tell him he was his father.

'Why, sure,' Matt said, looking at Rile and prodding him in the chest. When he spoke it was with a youthful excitement. 'Willy ran off but he knows we didn't shoot the driver.'

'Then we have to find him,' Delta said.

'He ran off again after the gunfight with King's men,' Matt said. 'I saw him go.'

'Ran off like a yellow rat,' Rile chipped in.

'Then we have to find him,' Delta repeated.

Steve stood up and worked a kink out of his neck. 'If this supposition of yours is correct,' he said, 'then King's probably got Willy tucked away somewhere or maybe he's killed him already.'

'That's as maybe,' Delta said. 'But we have to find out. If King's got him and if he's alive we'll have to get him.'

'And how do you suggest we do that?' Steve asked. 'King surrounds himself with heavily armed men.'

'We'll find a way,' Delta insisted. 'Whatever happens we have to find this man. The way I read this he could vindicate these two *hombres* here.'

NINETEEN

It had taken some time to persuade Matt and his *amigo*, Rile, that coming clean was the best course of action; finding Willy and proving that they had nothing to do with the killing of the driver would, Delta and Steve both maintained, cast doubt on the rest of King's claims. The only other option was for the two men to embark on the life of fugitives and that was not something that was particularly appealing. The robbery had been born out of bravado more than anything else; King wasn't exactly a popular figure in the area and Matt said it had seemed like justice to hit him.

King had robbed and cheated enough people in his time and it was poetic justice for some of it to be snatched back. Even Rile, who looked on the life of an outlaw with something of a romantic eye, had to agree that if they could keep the money they had stolen and get away without any charges, that would be something fine indeed. That would make them heroes around Hayes as well as further afield when the story got around, as it was likely to do. That was important to Rile: building a legend for himself. There was also the fact that he never wanted to go back to jail again and if everything worked out here they might be able to end up keeping the money and getting away totally free.

They had covered maybe ten miles when they came across King's men. Delta spotted them first, little more than specks in the distance, but he kept on riding towards the men, ordering the others to do likewise. He told Matt and Rile to hide their weapons in their saddle-bags and ride between him and Steve, as if they were under arrest and being taken into town to face justice. Now, when he called them to a stop besides a slow-flowing river, they watched the four riders come across the meadow and pull to a halt on the other side. There was perhaps twenty feet of river between the two groups of men and to a man they all sat there upon their horses, unsure what to do next.

Delta looked at both Matt and Rile, telling them not to make a move, to go along with what he was about to say.

'We're taking these two into Hayes,' he shouted. 'We've both been deputized by Sheriff Masters and these two men are our prisoners.'

The four men on the other side of the river seemed unsure of who was to take charge and they discussed something in hushed tones before one of them, a large, powerfully built man who went by the name of Tom Stark, broke away from the other three men and moved his horse forward to the river's edge.

'We've been looking for these two bandits ourselves,' he shouted back. 'I guess we'll ride back into town with you.'

Delta and Steve exchanged glances; it was clear that neither of them liked that idea. Matt and Rile didn't seem too keen themselves and each of them grew tense, knowing that a fight was brewing.

'We work alone,' Delta shouted back. 'We caught these two alone and we'll deliver them alone.'

'We don't want any share of the reward,' the man shouted back. 'Just want to make sure they reach town.'

'We work alone,' Delta repeated firmly. He looked back at his companions and nodded, telling them to stay calm, that he had the situation under control.

'We work for Maxwell King,' the man shouted. 'It's his money these men are wanted for robbing, men in his employ they killed. We come with you, stranger.'

Suddenly Delta felt a shooting pain in his chest and he pitched forward, falling from his horse.

Nerves were already frayed and Delta's sudden dive pretty much spooked everyone. Gunfire sounded before Delta had even hit the ground. The spokesman from King's band pulled his gun and shot without aiming but the bullet found a target, hitting Rile dead centre of his face, obliterating all features and sending a spray of crimson into the air as he was thrown backwards in the saddle, but he didn't fall off, his feet were trapped in their stirrups and he lay there upon the startled horse which broke into a gallop and ran off into the scrub behind them.

Matt fought to get his own horse under control, all the while sending off wild shots in the general direction of the men on the other side of the river. He could see Steve, kneeling on the ground, working the action on his Spencer rifle. Steve worked the rifle with great skill and sent off shot after shot at the men.

Matt looked around for Delta and saw him lying on the ground. He was clutching his left side and gritting his teeth. What had happened? Matt hadn't heard a gunshot before Delta had fallen, indeed it seemed as if he had fallen for no reason at all.

The horse came under some sort of control and Matt leapt to the ground. He crouched down and took aim at one of the men across the river, pulled the trigger and saw the man blown from his horse. Matt crawled across the ground, slugs slicing the air above him and got to Delta.

'You OK?' he asked, looking for a sign of an injury on the man, but there was none. A slug tore up the ground beside Delta and Matt threw himself on top of him, firing the Colt and hitting another of the men on the opposite side of the river. He fired again and cursed when he saw one of the horses keel over, a jagged chunk of its head shot clean off. He fired again and this time hit the man who had fallen from the horse.

'Good shooting, Matt,' Steve shouted and then displayed some mighty fine marksmanship himself as a slug from the Spencer took the last of King's men into the other world.

An eerie silence descended, the air hung heavy with the smell of cordite and fear.

'Goddamn bloodbath,' Steve said and stood up, peering across the river at the four dead men. He turned and saw that Matt was tending to Delta. He hadn't seen Rile's horse gallop off but he knew he'd been hit, had seen his head explode. He walked over to Matt and Delta.

Feeling was returning to Delta's left side, again his arm was tingling as if there were thousands upon thousands of ants crawling beneath the skin. He found his breathing was constricted, though, and the pain he had felt, like a stabbing in his chest, had been far more extreme than he'd ever experienced before. It had come suddenly, without any of the usual warnings such as feeling feverish or light-headed. He had been sure this was the big one, that this was the time when Weasel-face's bullet would finally do its work.

Damn you, Weasel-face, he cursed beneath his breath.

'We got them all,' Matt said.

Steve looked back over his shoulder at the battle-field on the other side of the river. Not only were the four men dead but their horses too.

'We sure did,' Steve said with a sardonic smile. 'All the King's horses and all the King's men.' He shook his head at the sheer senseless waste of life, then turned to look at Matt and Delta.

'Rile bought it too,' Matt said. 'His damn horse

ran off with him dead in the saddle.'

Steve nodded. That was pretty much the way he'd figured it had happened. He pointed his rifle at Delta, questioning.

'I'm OK,' Delta said. He tried to lift himself but he couldn't, his arms and legs felt as weak as those of a newborn. 'Help me up, I'll be OK in a minute.'

Matt and Steve did so, taking an arm each and lifting him to his feet.

'What the hell happened?' Steve asked.

'Give me a moment,' Delta said. 'Let me catch my breath.'

'You sure don't look well, mister,' Matt said. He held Delta tightly. 'Your legs are giving away beneath you.'

'I'll be fine,' Delta said. 'I just need a moment is all.'

The two men manhandled him over to a tree and then sat him down, his back resting against the tree.

'Obliged,' Delta said and started the breathing exercises the doc had taught him. It all seemed so long ago now. 'I'll be fine in a moment.'

'This is a mess,' Matt said, pacing back and forth. Only now did the full gravity of the situation hit him. 'Rile's dead and four more of King's men. This is turning into a war.'

'This was self-defence,' Steve said. 'Those varmints shot first. We'll pile some rocks on them and send the sheriff to recover the bodies.'

'What about Rile?' Matt asked.

'We'll take a look-see,' Steve said. 'But there's no

telling where his horse went; it might not stop running until he's clean out of the territory, and we're going against time here. We need to get to Willy before King does.'

Matt shivered, wiped his brow, asked: 'What do we do now?'

'Nothing's changed,' Delta said and managed to stand up. The feeling had now fully returned to his left arm and his breathing was easier as once again he bounced back from the edge of death's abyss. 'We stick to the plan.'

'You crazy?' Matt swung on his feet to face him. 'What use are you? What happened to you back then?'

For a moment Delta felt he might tell the boy everything. Not only about the bullet he carried inside him but also about his parentage. Make him realize that the reason it was so all-fired important that they should sort this mess out was that he didn't want his son throwing his life away. It seemed the thing to do. His own life was almost over, and he so wanted the boy to acknowledge him as his pa before he drew his final breath. But once more he kept the truth buckled up inside him alongside that fatal bullet.

In the end, though, he said nothing and merely changed the subject. He walked around as he spoke, as if to show that whatever had been wrong with him had now passed and he was once again fully fit.

'These men attacked us,' Delta said. 'They were acting on King's orders and trying to prevent us from returning to town and uncovering the truth about what's going on here. Nothing's changed. We find this Willy guy and prove you didn't kill the wagon driver.'

For a long while Steve looked at Delta without saying anything, obvious concern in his eyes. Then, deciding whatever was wrong with the man was his own business, he slapped Matt on the back, said: 'He's right, Matt. Nothing's changed.'

TWENTY

After covering the bodies of King's men with rocks and dirt, and failing to find Rile they rode on, then decided to split up at Four Forks, equidistant between the Big J and town.

They decided that it was still too much of a risk for them all to ride into town. They were pretty much sure that it was actually King or someone working on his orders who had been responsible for the killing of the wagondriver. It was felt that if they just rode in King would start a shoot out and then think up a reason afterwards. If he were guilty of the driver's murder then he would need to get Matt out of the way.

In the end they decided that Steve would ride into town alone and bring the sheriff out to Etta's place, while Matt and Delta rode on ahead to the relative safety of the ranch. With the sheriff onside they would have a better chance of running down Willy's whereabouts and if King was holding the man then the sheriff would be able to demand to talk to him.

It had to be Steve who went. Both Steve and Matt were too worried to trust Delta with the job, after what had happened to him earlier. Delta had given no satisfactory explanation as to what exactly had caused him to pitch forward out of his saddle, provoking the gun battle with King's men, and although neither Matt nor Steve said anything they were both concerned it could happen again. Happen at any moment.

'Bring the sheriff out to Etta's,' Delta said and took the makings from his shirt pocket. He quickly put together a smoke.

'Sure,' Steve said. 'And you watch out for the kid in the meantime.'

'I sure will.'

'I can look after myself,' Matt protested.

'Sure you can,' Delta said. 'Come on, let's be going. Good luck, Steve.'

Steve smiled, a grin that made the years fall from him. He seemed now to be enjoying himself.

'Luck don't come into it,' he said, and with that he spurred his horse into a gallop, leaving Matt and Delta in his dust cloud.

They both watched Steve vanish into the distance, then Delta started his own horse towards the valley where many years ago he had started the ranch with Etta. Matt spurred his own horse and kept it level with Delta's.

'You know your way around these parts,' Matt said, not a question but a statement of the obvious.

'I sure do.'

'From when you were here before?'

Delta nodded. 'There's been some changes,' he said. 'But the landscape is much the same as it's always been.'

'Is that when you knew my ma?'

Again Delta nodded but this time he said nothing.

For some time they rode on in silence, neither of them uttering a word, but for Delta the silence was deafening. He could hear what Matt would be thinking; sense the questions that would inevitably be churning around in his young mind. His imagination would be working overtime as he tried to work out the connection between this man and his ma.

'How do you know my ma?' Matt asked as they drove the horses across a shallow stream and entered the thin woodland that bordered the Big J property.

Delta didn't know how to answer that. He wasn't at all sure what he could say. Should he tell the boy that he was his pa? It was what he truly wanted to do but he didn't think he had the right to tell him here and now. He'd need to speak with Etta before he did so. Maybe she didn't want Matt to know, figuring the past was best left dead and gone.

'I passed through here once,' Delta said after some moments.

'And got to know my ma?'

'You know the big barn?'

'Yeah.'

'Well, I built that, and the fence that stops the cattle wandering up into the hills, I put that up too.'

'You used to work for my ma?'

Delta looked at his son and smiled. Worked for Etta, he figured that wasn't too far from the truth.

'That I did,' he said and spurred his horse on. 'Come on. Your ma'll be worried senseless for news.'

Matt hung back. The man called Delta bothered him in a way he couldn't understand. He had the strange feeling that there was something obvious here that he was missing, but for the life of him he couldn't figure out what that was. Still, the strange feeling persisted and he found himself caring deeply for this strange man. It was all on some instinctive level but he felt a connection with the man, almost a kinship.

Steve felt the need of a cool beer before seeing the sheriff and after tethering his horse he went through the batwings of the Double Diamond. There were only a few people in the saloon and Steve was thankful it was so quiet. A quick beer to revive his aching throat, he told himself, and then he'd go straight to Sheriff Masters.

Harvey, the barkeep, spotted Steve at the counter, came over, wiped his hands on his apron and smiled.

'What can I get you?'

'Just a beer, Harv.'

The barkeep poured the beer and slid the glass across the counter to Steve.

'Was a time when you cowboys used to push the boat out,' Harvey grumbled. 'How a man's supposed to make a living I do not know.'

'You do OK.'

'Do I? Do I really?'

'Sure you do. Now quit grumbling and give me another beer.' Steve drained the glass and handed it back. It had quenched his thirst somewhat but he hadn't enjoyed it with the barkeep moaning away.

'I'll retire a rich man,' the barkeep said and handed Steve a fresh beer.

'I'd appreciate some peace and quiet,' Steve said, ignoring the sarcasm. It wasn't a request and Harvey took it for what it was. He muttered something about ungrateful customers and then wandered off to bother the card players in the far corner. It had been some time since they'd refreshed their glasses in any case, and he wasn't running a charity here.

Steve sipped the beer, figuring he'd spend a few minutes over it and truly enjoy it before going off to see the sheriff. He turned his back against the counter and rested one heel against the foot rail. He could see out over the batwings and as he watched folk go about their business he felt himself relax.

Steve thought about the events of the last couple of days. First the stranger called Delta turns up and then, far from being a saddle tramp he is revealed as Matt's father. Then there was the robbery and the subsequent hunt for Matt, which had resulted in the gunfight and the death of another five men. The death toll was adding up and Steve had a feeling that before all this was over there would be even more to add to the tally.

Steve was almost done with the beer when he choked, coughing and spluttering beer over his shirtfront. The reason for this was there right in front of him – over the top of the batwings he could see the missing man, Willy. He had watched him for a moment before it had dawned on him who the man was. If Willy was hiding out he sure had a funny way of doing so: he was stumbling down the street as bold as you like.

Steve placed his glass on the counter and moved towards the batwings. He felt the butt of his Colt, figuring he would maybe have to hold Willy at gunpoint and march him to the sheriff's office. Or maybe he'd take him back out to the ranch, question him there and then call the sheriff in.

Steve pushed through the batwings and took a quick look up and down the street but, other than a few cowboys huddled in chat outside the land office and a group of women outside the Temperance Society building, the street was deserted. Well, apart from Willy who looked a little the worse for wear.

Steve crossed the street and went directly to Willy. He put an arm on the man's shoulder.

'I need to talk to you,' Steve said.

Willy looked at Steve through red-rimmed eyes. He was a little unsteady on his feet and he rocked gently.

'Tell King I ain't done nothing.' Willy was visibly trembling.

'Relax,' Steve said. 'I ain't nothing to do with that som-bitch. I just want to talk to you.'

'What about?'

'Oh just a little matter of a robbery.' Steve wrinkled his nose against the other man's putrid breath. He angled his head slightly so as to avoid the worst of Willy's exhalations.

'I need a drink,' Willy said. 'Can't think straight without a drink.'

'Looks like you've had enough already.'

Will grinned at that, revealing stained and chipped teeth.

'Begging Willy's pardon,' he said. 'But Willy could certainly do with another.'

'Come on,' Steve grabbed him by the arm. 'Let's get out of the street and we'll see about getting you something.'

Steve heard footsteps approaching but it was too late to react. He tried to spin on his feet, to see who it was who had come up behind them but he was suddenly pitched forward by a blinding blow to the back of head that rattled his teeth. He knew he'd been hit with something; the butt of a gun most likely, and he threw his hands out as he hit the dirt. Pain rebounded within his skull, which felt like it was due to explode.

When a man gets hit forcefully over the head confusion inevitably follows. Now this was no exception, but in the brief moment left to him before he slipped into unconsciousness Steve saw two men leading – scrub that – they were practically dragging Willy off.

More of King's men, no doubt.

TWENTY-ONE

Etta's mouth dropped open as she saw Delta and Matt riding towards the main enclosure. She ran to meet them, concern evident in her eyes. Where was Steve? What had happened to him?

'Matt,' she said, then she took her son in an embrace as soon as he had dismounted. A couple of ranch hands appeared and led Matt's and Delta's horses off to the stables.

Matt pushed his mother away and blushed in embarrassment. He cast a glance at Delta and smiled weakly.

'I'm fine, Ma,' he said. 'Let's go inside to talk.' Without waiting for them Matt walked off towards the ranch house.

'Did you tell him?' Etta asked, whispering to Delta. 'About him being my son?'

'Yes.'

'No.' Delta sighed. 'I didn't tell him.'

'Are you going to?'

'I'm not sure. What do you think?'

'Beats me.'

'Come on,' Delta said. 'Let's go talk.'

They both walked towards the ranch house to where Matt waited in the doorway. The kid watched them come, aware of how comfortable they seemed to be in each other's company. That bothered the kid somewhat but again he wasn't really sure why.

Once inside they all went into the kitchen and Etta put a fresh pot of coffee on the stove. She busied herself with making the beverage while Matt and Delta sat down at the long table that dominated the room.

'Well,' she asked, 'is anyone going to tell me what's going on?'

Delta told it. About him and Steve coming across Matt and Rile and about the gunfight with King's men. Then he pointed out that Matt, whilst responsible for the robbery, had not shot the wagon driver, nor had any of his partners. Indeed, when they had ridden off, whooping at hollering at their sudden wealth, both the driver and the shotgun rider had been alive and well. Though the shotgun, a man named Willy (whom Etta said she knew), had fled when the robbery started.

Delta then went on and outlined his suspicion that King had actually killed the driver, maybe in a sudden fury upon learning about the robbery. That was why Steve had gone on into town, to bring the sheriff over so that they could find out what had really happened. It was thought the key was with the missing man, that he would be able to prove that

Matt and his partners had nothing to do with any murder. Maybe, Delta reasoned, if they did that then no charges over the robbery would be forthcoming and it would be King rather than Matt who faced the hangman. At least that way Matt wouldn't have to live the life of an outlaw. And if the worst did come to the worst then Delta would ensure that Matt escaped. That he was certain of and Etta knew he meant it.

'So what do we do now?' Etta asked, joining them at the table.

'We wait,' Delta said. 'It's all we can do. As soon as Steve returns with the sheriff we'll set about tracking this Willy character down.

'Well, until then,' Matt said, getting up and stretching wearily, 'until he does I'm going to get myself some sleep. I feel as if I ain't slept in weeks and if I don't lie down soon I'm going to fall down.'

'You can sleep at a time like this?' Etta looked at her son, a frown on her face.

'Nothing else I can do,' Matt said and wandered off for the bedroom he hadn't slept in for a long while. He guessed that when this was all over, if it worked out OK, he's spend more time at home, working on the ranch and less time running around with his friends playing at being bad men. Then it dawned on him that those friends were now dead, all of them. That simple fact, above all others, made him realize that the life of an outlaw was not as the dime novels depicted it.

'Let the boy sleep,' Delta advised. 'He sure looks

like he needs it.'

Etta sighed and sat in silence with her coffee until she heard Matt's bedroom door close. Then she looked Delta directly in the eye and shook her head.

'This is a mess,' she said.

'It is.'

'So what are you going to do? Are you going to tell Matt you're his pa?'

'Do you want me to?'

Etta shrugged. 'He seems to like you,' she said.

'Does he?'

'You can tell.' Etta reached across the table and took one of Delta's hands in her own. 'You can see the way he looks at you.'

Delta felt both awkward and thrilled at the feel of her hand within his own. He looked at her and at that moment it was as if he had never been away. He still knew the woman inside out and even if he hadn't spent the last twenty years with her it made not a difference. He'd always felt it with Etta, like they were kindred spirits and were meant to be together. Etta was a good-hearted woman and Delta felt an utter fool for turning his back on her all those years ago. In a perfect world that wouldn't matter and they would be able to get on with rekindling whatever it was they'd had between them, building a future together. Only, thanks to Weasel-face, Delta didn't have much of a future.

'He's a fine boy,' Delta said at last, and pulled his hand free of Etta's grasp. He sipped the bitter coffee and rubbed his face wearily in his hands.

'He reminds me of you,' Etta said. 'How you used to be.'

'I thank you for that,' Delta said. 'I haven't been much of a pa. Hell, I ain't been any kind of a pa, but there's one thing I can do for the boy. I'm going to make sure we clear all this up and he ain't going to face a rope or a life on the lam. That ain't no kind of life, having to outrun the law just to stay alive.'

'That's not for Matt,' Etta said.

'He won't live like that,' Delta said. 'That I can guarantee.'

Etta smiled.

She believed him.

Again silence descended between them and it was Delta who broke that silence.

'King's place,' he asked, 'it's about six miles south of here?'

Etta nodded.

And that was that and once again they both fell silent, each of them lost in private thoughts.

Matt woke a little after noon and went through to the kitchen to find his mother seated on the soft stool by the window. She was gazing out at the corral, watching the horses shuffling about in the lazy afternoon heat.

'Where's Delta?' Matt asked, startling his mother.

She turned and noticed he was wearing his gunbelt, which provoked a frown. She had never liked him wearing his guns in the house. It was a rule that Matt usually respected, but she didn't say anything this time.

'He's about the ranch somewhere,' Etta said. 'You want coffee, something to eat?'

'Later maybe,' Matt said and went outside in search of Delta.

Etta watched her son cross the corral and go first into one barn and then into another. Then he vanished from view as he went behind the ranch house. A few moments later he came back into view and ran towards the house.

'He's ridden out,' Matt said as he entered the kitchen. 'Mosey told me he went about an hour ago.'

Etta looked at her son. Delta hadn't told her he was leaving the ranch and had said he was going to make himself useful. Where had he gone? Suddenly it dawned on her and she knew without a doubt where it was he had gone. He had asked about the location of the King spread and she had told him. He ridden out there, with what purpose she wasn't quite clear, but then Delta had always been an ornery man and she had never truly understood him.

'Where's he gone?' Matt asked. 'And why isn't Steve back?'

'I don't know,' Etta said. 'He never told me he was leaving.'

That seemed to satisfy Matt for a moment and he stared out of the window. It was obvious he was on edge and Etta could see that he thought a lot of Delta. He didn't really know anything about him, had no idea that he was his father, but all the same he was deeply concerned about him.

'I think he might have ridden out to Maxwell King's place,' she said.

'I'm going after him,' Matt said and was almost out of the door when his mother called him back.

'Stay here, Matt,' she pleaded, then her voice took on a firmer edge. 'You stay here.'

Matt looked his mother directly in the eyes and shook his head.

'I'm going, Ma,' he said.

'No. Wait.'

Matt shook his head. 'I'm going.'

'Then I'm coming with you.'

'No.'

'I'm coming with you or I'll ride out after you,' Etta insisted.

Matt looked at his mother and he knew it was futile to argue further.

TWENTY-TWO

It turned out that Steve didn't have to go looking for the sheriff.

The sheriff found him.

The sheriff, along with two other men, helped Steve to his feet but Steve pushed them away and fell back to his knees. He retched and vomited in the dirt, which made the throbbing in his skull even worse. He felt the back of his head and found it was moist with blood. There was also a goose egg that felt like a triple yoker.

'You OK?' the sheriff asked.

'Just dandy.' Steve spoke through gritted teeth. 'Just fine and dandy.' He wiped his mouth on the back of his hand and then cleaned the hand in the dirt. He managed to get to his feet and kicked dirt over his vomit.

'What happened?'

Steve looked at the sheriff and then at the two men with him.

'I think we need to talk in your office,' he said.

The sheriff nodded and led the way, while Steve followed and the other two men, although crestfallen at being left out of things, went about their business.

It took maybe ten minutes for Steve to tell the sheriff the entire story, but the sheriff took twice that time asking questions. Steve knew Jake Masters well and liked him, found him a good man, someone who really did believe in the law. Maxwell King's standing in the territory would not sway him at all from doing his duty.

'So you see,' Steve concluded, 'only Willy can prove that Matt's gang wasn't responsible for the killing of the driver. Which is why I guess King's men snatched him and pounded me half-senseless.' He was sure that it was indeed men working on King's behalf who had come up behind him and struck him. He was also positive that they were now holding Willy against his will and that the old drunk didn't have long before King silenced him for ever. With Willy gone there would be no way of proving Matt's innocence in the murder of the driver.

The sheriff sucked on his pipe, staring at Steve through a thick cloud of smoke. He sat back in his chair, his feet up on his desk.

'Can you ride?' he asked.

Steve ran a hand over the back of his head. 'Sure,' he said. He still felt a little hazy but he guessed he'd be OK.

'Then I guess we'd better take a ride out to King's place,' the sheriff said. 'But afterwards I'm going to have to ride out to Etta's and bring Matt in.'

'I know that,' Steve said. 'But I figure that if we get to Willy then maybe things'll look a little different.'

The sheriff stood up. He had known Etta for many years and he hoped that that would prove true. Matt, whilst a little headstrong and wild, certainly wasn't a cold-blooded killer.

'We'll see,' the sheriff said, and led the way out into the blinding afternoon sunshine.

Delta tethered his horse to one of the cottonwoods that surrounded King's impressive-looking ranch house, and moved forward on foot. He wanted to remain hidden, to take a look around.

King's ranch house was built, like Etta's place, in a deep valley, which allowed Delta plenty of scope to stay hidden whilst he tried to figure out what was happening. He was standing on a rise, watching a thin trail of smoke coming from King's chimney, when he saw two men dragging another man between them towards the ranch house. The man being manhandled wasn't exactly fighting, but it was clear that he wasn't going with the men of his own free will.

Willy, Delta guessed.

So King had got him. The only man who could prove Matt's innocence in the murder of the driver was currently being pulled and pushed and dragged towards King's ranch house.

There was no doubt that it was Willy with the two cowboys below. It was the only thing that made sense and he also knew that it was likely the man would end up dead pretty damn soon. If King had in fact been responsible for the murder of the driver he wouldn't balk at gunning down this other man in order to pin it all on Matt.

'Got to free Willy,' Delta mumbled. Talking to himself was one of the little habits he had developed during a life spent in the saddle.

He crouched down, remaining hidden for some time after the two men had taken the other man into the ranch house. He wondered what was going on behind the closed doors and how long he had before the man called Willy was disposed of. He remained like that for a few minutes, debating the best course of action; then he decided that direct action was the only option. He started down the incline towards the ranch house. He thought better of it though when he saw a group of men huddled together outside the large bunkhouse. It was only a matter of time before he was seen and the alarm was sounded. There was no way of approaching the ranch house without being seen and he figured he would have to ride on in there, go in quickly, taking advantage of the confusion and try and snatch the man called Willy before anyone knew what was happening. That couldn't be done on foot, and so he made his way back to his horse.

Delta mounted up and followed the tree-lined pathway that led down to the ranch house. He was hoping to get within twenty or thirty feet of the ranch before he was spotted and then send his horse into a gallop. The ranch had been built in a mixture of the

Western and Mexican styles: the lower section was constructed from adobe blocks while the upper floors were of a dark-stained timber. There was a large window at the centre of the front of the house with the main door beside it.

In contrast to the grand ranch house the bunkhouse was, though admittedly large, a far more basic building, which had been constructed from logs. There were several other wooden buildings – stables, barns and a large storage shed. There was also a windmill situated alongside the large corral.

Delta figured the large window would be the most effective way to enter the house quickly, get in, snatch Willy and then get out before anyone really had a chance to react. He'd shoot the glass out and then take his horse straight through the newly created entrance; it was sure big enough. He was hoping the ensuing chaos and confusion would give him a chance to get to Willy with as little gunfire as possible, but if anyone got in his way then he was fully prepared to gun them down. The ends, he figured, justified the means.

It was risky, Delta realized, but then he reminded himself of that old bullet snuggled up inside him: best not forget that. If he failed and took another bullet then he had nothing to lose. If he succeeded and in the chaos managed to get away with Willy then there was everything to gain. He was determined to clear Matt and prevent him from having to live the life of an outlaw, which would go some way to redeem him for his failings as a father. The fact that until recently he didn't even know of the boy's existence meant nothing. He hadn't been much of a man to Etta and even less of a father to the boy.

So far so good, Delta thought. He had reached the level ground and was now heading towards the main enclosure and still he hadn't been spotted. He didn't think this would last for much longer.

TWENTY-THREE

Etta didn't ride sidesaddle; she could handle a horse as well as any man and Matt made no allowances for his mother as he galloped at breakneck speed for King's spread. Not that it mattered, for Etta, mounted on a magnificent paint pony, was with him all the way. There was one tricky moment when Etta's mount seemed to lose its footing, almost throwing Etta, but she held on and the horse somehow managed to right itself.

They were within perhaps a mile of King's spread when they saw Steve and the sheriff coming from the opposite direction.

Matt looked at his mother, as if unsure what to do. Would the sheriff arrest him on sight? Would it all end here with him being dragged off to jail, facing charges of robbery and murder? That however wasn't Matt's chief concern and he would quite happily take what was coming to him just as long as they made sure the man called Delta was safe.

'Matt, stop,' Etta shouted and pulled on the reins of the paint.

Matt did so and sat there in the saddle, watching Steve and the lawman approach. He wiped the sweat from his brow with the back of a hand.

'What's happening here?' the sheriff asked as he and Steve pulled their own mounts to a stop beside Matt and Etta. He looked at the kid, then frowned. 'You've brought a whole heap of trouble on yourself here.'

'Yes, sir,' Matt said and left it at that.

'Jake,' Etta said, 'Matt didn't kill anyone.'

The sheriff looked at her with concern in his eyes. He could understand how she felt. Although women had always been a mystery to him, the maternal instinct was something he could understand. Even wild critters felt an instinctive need to protect their young.

'Steve's told me the kid's side of things,' he said. 'But even if that's true there's still blood on the kid's hands. Maybe not all of it directly but it was the robbery of King's money that started this whole shooting-match.'

'Where's Delta?' Steve put in before Matt could say anything. He had noticed the steely glint in the boy's eyes as the sheriff spoke and he knew his damn temper was about to get the better of him.

'He's gone after King,' Matt said.

'Alone?' Steve asked.

Both Etta and Matt nodded.

'Who does he think he is?' Steve asked. 'Arkansas Smith?'

Etta smiled, weakly. Arkansas Smith: she knew the

name of course. It ranked up there alongside Wyatt Earp, General Custer, Billy the Kid and others of like fame. Matt had a dime novel at home about the man. She seemed to remember it was titled *King of the Colt* and written by some purple prose-loving hack named G. M. Dobbs. Etta had read a page or two herself before tossing it aside. The book had claimed that Arkansas Smith walked like an ox, ran like a fox, swam like an eel and fought like a demon. He could spout like a volcano, make love like a wild bull and swallow an Indian whole without choking.

Mind you, she supposed, that pretty much summed up Delta Rose.

'What's he thinking of?' the sheriff asked. 'What's he got in mind?'

'Beats me,' Matt said. 'He didn't tell us he was going. Just upped and left.'

The sheriff looked at the kid. He wondered whether he knew that the man called Delta was his father: whether anyone had told him, but he didn't think so. Steve had told him the boy had no idea of his paternal parentage but he wasn't at all sure whether Etta or Delta were going to tell him.

'You still have some questions to answer,' the sheriff said, pointing a finger towards Matt. 'So don't you even think of running off when all this is over.'

'I won't,' Matt said. 'You have my word on that.'

That satisfied the sheriff and he nodded.

'Then I guess the thing to do is get to King's place as quickly as we can.' He looked at Etta and for a moment considered telling her to stay here while they handled this, but he knew he would be wasting his time. Etta could be a stubborn woman and when she set her mind on something there was just no reasoning with her.

Steve then told them what had happened in town, about finding Willy and then being struck on the back of the head by person or persons unknown, but it seemed pretty certain that whoever had struck Steve had been in King's employ. This was the reason they were riding out to King's place; to get hold of Willy and hear his side of what happened during the robbery.

'King'll kill him,' Matt said presently.

The sheriff's horse was kicking the ground, snorting and he pulled it under control. The damn thing was getting restless.

'That's a possibility that's crossed my mind,' he said. 'I wouldn't put it past the som-bitch in any case.'

'Then let's get going,' Matt said and spurred his horse back into a gallop.

The foursome rode like the wind, Matt taking a slight lead but the other three kept up with him and together they galloped straight ahead into the unknown.

·

Maxwell King looked at Willy through contemptuous eyes. The old man, held firm by Cade and a ranch hand, looked terrified. He was dirty, unshaven and his eyes, usually sunk back in his pallid face, were now wide and staring as the Englishman came towards him.

'Why'd you run off?' King asked.

Willy shook his head, unable to answer.

King sent a powerful blow into Willy's stomach and the old man groaned as the air was pushed from his lungs. The two cowboys held him steady though and King delivered another blow to his stomach. Willy almost passed out but he remained conscious, coughing and spluttering for breath.

'Sit him down,' King said but not before he had hit him one more time. 'You disappoint me, Willy. I expect loyalty from men who work for me, not treachery and cowardliness.'

Willy said nothing but not because he had nothing to say, more because he was still unable to speak. He had urinated in his pants and there was the coppery taste of blood in his mouth.

'You left Clift to face the bandits alone,' King said, pacing the small room at the rear of the house where they had taken Willy. They were unlikely to be disturbed here and the men outside wouldn't to be able to hear anything that went on. He lit a cigar and drew hard, inhaling the smoke. 'Clift was your friend and you left him to the mercy of the bandits. You left him to face his death alone.'

Willy shook his head, his terrified eyes looking at the cowboy each side of him and then directly at King. He tried to speak but all that emerged was a gurgled gasp. Clift had been alive when he'd run off and from his hiding-place he had seen that the man was still alive when the bandits rode off with the strongbox from the wagon. Maybe he should have emerged then, Willy thought, but at the time he'd been frantic with fear and was unsure how Clift would react if he suddenly emerged from hiding. He was, after all, supposed to have been riding shotgun and had a duty to protect the money, but then no one thought anyone would have had the nerve to rob from Maxwell King. He tried once again to speak but was unable to form the words.

'I ought to kill you,' King said. 'That's no more than you deserve.'

Cade and the other man cast a glance at each other, fully expecting King to pull a weapon and shoot Willy dead there and then.

'I . . . I. . . .' Willy managed but his words were silenced when King sent a stinging blow across his face with the back of his hand. Willy cried then, sobbed like a child.

King looked at the old man, as if contemplating what to do with him. For several uncomfortable and silent moments he kept the man trapped in his gaze, then he pulled out the derringer he carried concealed in a shoulder holster. He pointed the weapon straight at Willy's face, held it there for a moment, then smiled and lowered it.

'I'm going to spare you,' King said. 'But only so you can testify against those who killed Clift.'

Willy again shook his head frantically. 'Begging Willy's pardon,' he said. 'But Clift weren't killed by no bandits.'

King replied with another stinging blow to the man's face. He stood there for a moment, smoking the cigar and watching Willy, taking some enjoyment from the old man's pain.

'I don't think you rightly understand what's happening here,' King said, then looked at Cade. 'Hit him.'

Cade punched the old man with a fist of iron, hard knuckles tearing the skin at the side of his face. The old man yelped and then his head fell forward as unconsciousness mercifully took him.

'Bring him round,' King said. 'We'll try again.'

TWENTY-FOUR

Delta couldn't believe his luck but he had managed to reach the point where the land levelled out and he was only feet from the entrance to the main enclosure when he was eventually noticed. Sure enough, King's men had all seen him now and were peering curiously in his direction. He kept the horse moving at a walking pace for the moment. Until someone came over to challenge him he would continue doing so.

He went through the gate, smiling at the oversized bullhorns that had been suspended on the cross-post. From what he had learned about King the man wouldn't know one end of a cow from the other.

Now one of King's cowboys was coming towards him and Delta took a deep breath. He placed the reins in his mouth and filled each hand with iron.

He kept the horse moving slowly, though. There was no need to create a panic until the very last moment. There was a cowboy coming towards him but thus far he hadn't seemed to notice anything out of the usual. Delta kept his hands down so that his guns wouldn't be visible.

Another few feet, he told himself.

Another few feet and then he'd start shooting.

Delta's eyes scanned from left to right. He was starting to gather attention now and there were men coming towards him from either side. Whatever was going to happen here today it was going to start pretty damn soon.

'Hey mister,' a cowboy shouted and stepped into Delta's path. The man noticed the reins in Delta's mouth, then his eyes went down to the guns in Delta's hands. He reached for his own weapon.

Delta simultaneously sent a shot over his head and kicked the horse into a gallop. He shot at the house, seeing the windows suddenly shattered in a hail of glass that glittered and flashed in the sunlight. As he had expected there was general chaos and no one had returned fire by the time he sent his horse crashing through the opening created when he'd shot the window out.

The horse was terrified but well trained and Delta had it under control as he pulled it to a stop inside the house. He jumped from the beast just as a man carrying a rifle came through the door. The rifle cracked and a slug passed by Delta's face.

Delta shot back, hitting the man in the gut and sending him flailing back through the doorway. The man was dead before he hit the floor, a large gaping wound in the centre of his stomach, through which gore bubbled like a geyser.

Delta coughed and spluttered as dust and ceiling plaster fell around him. He fired two shots back out of the window in order to keep the cowboys outside from getting too brave. He went through the door, stepping over the dead man, and saw two other men at the other end of the corridor. Delta threw himself to the floor just as two bullets whizzed above him and punched into the wall.

He shot back twice. The first slug took one man in his chest, sending him crashing backwards to slide down the wall behind him. The other hit the second man in the head and sent a chunk of his skull into the air with a burst of crimson. Both men had now left the game.

Delta sensed there were men behind him; he knew they had come through the window and were in the room he had just vacated. He sent several shots into the doorway, hoping to hold them back. Then he reloaded each weapon before running down the corridor and heading through another door.

He saw two men dragging an old man between them. The old man was only semi-conscious and Delta recognized him as Willy.

'Let him go,' Delta said, holding both weapons centred on the men.

The two men moved as one, throwing the old man towards Delta, but he fell flat on the floor, unable to move. Then both men pulled their own weapons and started shooting.

Delta felt a slug graze the side of his face and immediately warm blood trickled down his skin. He hit the floor just as another bullet – only this time coming from behind him – went over his head. He was caught in the crossfire and he immediately turned and shot the man behind him. Another man came through the door and Delta shot him too. He turned his attention back to the men in front of him. He shot without aiming but the bullet found home and one of the men's faces disappeared in a cloud of blood and bone. Delta laid himself over the semi-conscious old man and fired again, but he saw the wall splinter behind his target and another bullet powered into the floor besides him, uncomfortably close.

Delta fired again. This time he hit the man but didn't kill him outright. The man slid to the floor, clutching a wound in his stomach through which his entrails protruded. The man clutched his innards in disbelief, trying to push them back into his stomach. Delta shot the man again, this time out of mercy, and the man left this world and his pain behind.

'Come on,' Delta said, pulling the old man to his feet.

'Begging Willy's pardon,' the old man said, looking at the carnage around him.

'Come on,' Delta said and half-dragged the man towards the front of the house. Another man came out of the doorway in front of him and Delta shot him immediately.

'Begging Willy's pardon,' the old man said again. 'Begging Willy's pardon.'

'Shut up.' Delta continued to drag the man

towards the front door, figuring this was now the safest way to leave the building. Not that anywhere was safe and the ranch had become a war zone.

Delta heard footsteps behind him and he quickened his pace, pulling the old man along with him. They had to get outside if they were to make a fight of it.

They reached the front door and Delta told the old man to keep low as he pulled the door open. But no gunfire came at them and once more he grabbed the old man and pulled him through the doorway.

Now the gunfire started and Delta, dragging the old man with him, ran for the cover of the wall. Gunfire sounded like thunder, coming from all directions. The ground around spat dust as bullets missed their targets and tore up the dirt. Delta sent off a few shots behind him and continued running.

They reached the wall, which was waist height, and Delta helped the old man over.

'Keep down,' he said. 'Take cover.'

The old man didn't need telling twice and as soon as he was over the wall he hit the ground and remained there. Lying prone, his hands over his head, he mumbled a prayer over and over.

Delta fired off wildly behind him, emptying both of his guns, then he leapt on to the wall. A sudden sharp pain struck in his chest, taking his breath from him and he arched his back before falling face first on to the ground behind the old man.

As soon as he hit the ground he tried to reload his guns but it was a major effort and he felt the numbness starting in his left side. Through gritted teeth he used his right hand, resting both pistols between his legs as he slid shells into their chambers.

'Can you shoot?' he asked the old man.

Willy nodded.

'Take one,' Delta said as a bullet ricocheted off the wall, whistling through the air but the sound becoming lost amongst the roar of further gunfire.

Willy grabbed a gun but didn't make any effort to get up from the relative safety of the wall that was acting as a barricade.

Delta managed to peer over the wall; he saw that there was a small army out there. More than dozen men had taken up positions in and around the ranch house and were ready to cut both Delta and the old man down the moment they showed themselves.

'You were the shotgun rider on King's wagon?' Delta asked. He felt feverish and he had to grit his teeth. Not now, he thought. Now was not the time for Weasel-face's bullet to claim him. Not when there were so many others out there with his name on.

'I was.' Willy nodded, then crouched down lower when a hail of gunfire struck the wall. 'The robbery weren't my fault.'

'The driver?' Delta asked, through teeth that were gritted so tightly his jaw ached. The paralysis was taking over again and he knew that in a moment he would have little if any control over his body. 'Who killed him?'

Willy was totally confused. King had been taking a similar line of questioning with him and now, as then, he had no answers.

'No one,' he said. 'No one killed Clift.'

That was all Delta needed to know and, despite their current impossible situation, he smiled. He'd known it all along but this verified it. Matt was no cold-blooded killer.

'King killed Clift,' Delta said and then screamed as a great pain welled up inside him. It felt as if someone had reached inside him and was squeezing his heart. He arched his back and slipped away into blackness, thinking as he went that this was it.

'Mister,' Willy shook Delta, 'are you OK?'

But there was no answer.

TWENTY-FIVE

As soon as they heard the gunfire, the sheriff took the lead; he pulled his own gun and tried to get as much extra speed out of his horse as possible. It sounded like a full-scale battle was going on up ahead.

'Keep back,' Steve ordered Etta and filled his own hand, as did Matt and they all tried to spur as much speed as possible from their respective mounts. From here they reached King's ranch in mere minutes but it felt like hours and the closer they got the stronger the smell of cordite became.

Gunfire greeted them, bullets whizzed over their heads. The sheriff dismounted first. He hit the ground in a crouch and fired back towards the ranch house.

'Hold your fire,' he shouted. 'This is Sheriff Masters. This is the law.'

Law didn't seem to count none and more gunfire came from the ranch house. Steve hugged the ground beside the sheriff and returned several shots with his rifle.

Etta had dismounted and took shelter behind a fence. She tried to peer into the main enclosure to see what was happening, but there was no sign of Delta. What the hell had happened here?

Matt saw Delta first. He set his horse towards the ranch house and, ignoring the bullets that set the air around him on fire, he continued forward. The horse jumped the fence of the enclosure and Matt kept it galloping towards the small dividing wall behind which Delta was hiding with the old man.

Matt reached them and jumped from his horse, allowing the beast to run off away from the line of fire. A bullet chipped the wall behind him and Matt fired at the rifle flash. He saw a man fall from the bunkhouse roof.

'Delta,' Matt said and knelt down beside him. He looked at the old man, Willy, with questioning eyes but all he received was a shrug of the shoulders. There was blood on the side of Delta's face, a deep gash where a bullet had grazed him but other than that he didn't seem to have been hit.

Delta's eyes opened and he started gasping for breath. He was still alive, which surprised the old man as well as himself. He tried to get to his feet but there was still considerable weakness in his left side and his limbs didn't seem to work.

'The old man proves your innocence,' Delta said. 'You've got to get him to safety.'

'I ain't leaving you,' Matt said and had to duck when further gunfire chipped stone off the top of the wall.

Matt looked across to where Steve and the sheriff were pinned down. They were returning fire when they could but for the most part they had to lie there and keep their mouths chewing the dirt. He could see no sign of his mother, which reassured him a little because it meant she had hidden herself away somewhere out of the line of fire. This was no good and could go on for ever. As long as they kept their heads down King's men couldn't hit them, but nor could they strike back.

The stalemate had to be broken.

Matt might have one chance. If he could get over to wall at its furthest point and come up at the ranch house from behind he could maybe even things up a little. Maybe King's men wouldn't be so willing to fight if their advantage was taken from them.

Matt looked at Delta and the old man, noticed that they were both packing iron.

'Cover me,' he said and before either of them could protest he leapt over the wall and ran for dear life, heading for the rear of the ranch house. Bullets whizzed around him but no one could get a clear shot at him without getting their heads shot off either by Delta and the old man or by Steve and the sheriff.

Matt reached the ranch house and threw himself against the wall. From here he could see several of King's men down behind the fence that ran alongside the house. He fired twice, killing two of them and had to duck back behind the wall when a hail of gunfire answered him.

This opened things up a bit and allowed Steve and the sheriff to advance towards the main enclosure. The dirt spat up besides the sheriff and the lawman fired.

A split second later another man fell from the roof.

'Hold your fire,' the sheriff ordered.

Incredibly it worked and one by one King's men stood up, dropping their weapons and raising their hands. The fight had become two-sided and that wasn't to their liking.

Matt waited a moment to make sure it was no trick, but all the fight had gone out of the men and he watched as the sheriff and Steve lined the cowboys up against the wall. He holstered his gun and wiped his brow. They had Willy, and so would be able to prove that he, Matt, hadn't killed the wagon driver. King's money was still hidden away safely and Matt figured that King wouldn't need it for a long, long time, if ever. If it turned out that King had been responsible for his own driver's death then he could very well face the rope.

Matt ran back over to Delta and the old man and he noticed his mother coming towards them from the opposite direction.

It was over.

TWENTY-SIX

'Where's King?' Sheriff Masters asked. There were more than a dozen cowboys, all unarmed, standing waiting for instructions from the lawman. Steve stood, keeping his rifle trained on the men.

'I'm here,' King yelled from the ranch house.

Delta, now that full mobility had returned, walked over and stood next to the sheriff. He gave the lawman a small smile, as if to congratulate him on a job well done. Matt remained with Steve and his mother, who were tending to the old man's injuries. Poor Willy had taken quite a beating at the hands of King's men.

'Well, come out,' the sheriff yelled towards the ranch house. 'And keep your hands up where I can see them.'

'I'm coming out,' King yelled. 'Don't nobody shoot.'

'Just get a move on,' the sheriff said and rolled his eyes.

King came through the doorway and Delta took

two steps forward, unable to believe what he was seeing. The man named Maxwell King was the man who had haunted his dreams these last few years, the man he thought of as Weasel-face.

'I'm sure we can clear all this up,' King said and continued walking towards the sheriff.

Delta stared at King, knowing that this was the man who had killed him a couple of years back. And now this same man had tried to blame Matt for his own wrongdoing.

'Weasel-face,' Delta said and raised his gun as King looked at him. For a moment the Englishman looked confused, then recollection dawned and a look of sheer terror crossed his face.

'Drop your weapon,' the sheriff said. 'King's in my custody and if you gun him down now it'll be cold-blooded murder. You'll hang for it.'

Delta didn't lower his gun but kept it trained firmly on the trembling King. He looked first at the sheriff and then at Etta and the others. His eyes fell last of all on Matt and he smiled.

'Do well, son,' he said and pulled the trigger, sending Weasel-face to hell.

Delta watched King hit the ground, watched him squirm and then lie perfectly still.

'You killed me,' he said. He dropped his weapon to the ground and looked at the sheriff. He felt the bullet shift inside him and then a stabbing pain, far greater than ever before. But he stood there, immobile, then he closed his eyes and fell to the ground.

Dead.